P9-CQY-280

PRAISE FOR DON PENDLETON

COPP IN THE DARK

"Copp's adventures don't lack for action. They might best be described as Spillane on speed."

—*The Florida Times-Union*

"Fast-paced . . ."

—*The Flint Journal*

COPP IN DEEP

"Reads like an express train . . . Pendleton knows how to keep us turning the pages."

—*Publishers Weekly*

"[Pendleton] mines another bestselling vein with the cases of ex-cop/private eye Joe Copp, the toughest operator this side of Mike Hammer."

—*ALA Booklist*

"Pendleton's spare, rugged prose is a perfect fit."

—*St. Louis Post-Dispatch*

"Pendleton is the master."

—*Kirkus Reviews*

Also by Don Pendleton

COPP ON FIRE
COPP IN DEEP
*COPP ON ICE

Published by
HarperPaperbacks

*coming soon

ATTENTION: ORGANIZATIONS AND CORPORATIONS

Most HarperPaperbacks are available at special quantity discounts for bulk purchases for sales promotions, premiums, or fund-raising. For information, please call or write:
Special Markets Department, HarperCollins Publishers, 10 East 53rd Street, New York, N.Y. 10022. Telephone: (212) 207-7528. Fax: (212) 207-7222.

DON PENDLETON

COPP IN THE DARK

HarperPaperbacks
A Division of HarperCollins*Publishers*

If you purchased this book without a cover, you should be aware that this book is stolen property. It was reported as "unsold and destroyed" to the publisher and neither the author nor the publisher has received any payment for this "stripped book."

This is a work of fiction. The characters, incidents, and dialogues are products of the author's imagination and are not to be construed as real. Any resemblance to actual events or persons, living or dead, is entirely coincidental.

HarperPaperbacks *A Division of* HarperCollins*Publishers*
10 East 53rd Street, New York, N.Y. 10022

Copyright © 1990 by Don Pendleton
All rights reserved. No part of this book may be used or reproduced in any manner whatsoever without written permission of the publisher, except in the case of brief quotations embodied in critical articles and reviews. For information address Donald I. Fine, Inc., 128 East 36th Street, New York, N.Y. 10016.

This book is published by arrangement with Donald I. Fine, Inc.

Cover illustration by Uldis Klavins
Cover photograph courtesy of the Bettmann Archive

First HarperPaperbacks printing: February 1992

Printed in the United States of America

HarperPaperbacks and colophon are trademarks of HarperCollins*Publishers*

10 9 8 7 6 5 4 3 2 1

For all the splendidly talented people everywhere who keep live theater alive and well, and who give so much to so many for so little. Please keep on.

". . . And the world will be better for this,
That one man, scorned and covered with scars,
Still strove, with his last ounce of courage,
To reach the unreachable stars!"

—Song lyric, "The Impossible Dream" ("The Quest")

Special thanks to George Champion, masterly voice of La Mancha on the Southern California stage, for his insights and valuable counsel.

CHAPTER 1

I HEARD A rustling movement and knew that someone had sat down behind me in the darkened lounge, but I had no other clues until she spoke in a soft little whisper almost at my ear. "Thank you for being so understanding."

I understood nothing. The place had been closed for over an hour. A door had been left open for me at the far side of the building and I'd found my way along a maze of dimly lit corridors to keep an appointment in the dark with a person I'd never met. I had come out of simple curiosity, responding to a murky message left on my telephone answering machine and because the appointed place is at my edge of the L.A. area and I had nothing else to do at three A.M. anyway.

It's a luxury hotel complex complete with several fine restaurants, a dinner theater and a lounge, various other diversions, and I knew the place.

"Please don't turn around," whispered the voice in the dark. "If you do, I'll have to leave." Obviously my mysterious prospective client had been waiting for me in the dark, concealed somewhere inside, because I would have seen her if she'd come in behind me from the softly lighted foyer.

I shrugged—for my own benefit, I guess—and said, "I'm comfortable. What's up?"

"I want to hire you."

"I gathered as much. For what?"

"What do you charge?"

"Depends on what or who I have to do. What's the job?'

"I'm in the show," she whispered. "In the cast, I mean *Man of La Mancha*. At the dinner theater next door."

I knew about it. It had been a long run, held over twice Saw it myself. I'm no critic but . . . I liked it. Mostly kids trying to get a start in professional theater but a lot of talent and enthusiasm to make up for the lack of experience

"That's a problem?" I asked her.

"Well, it's getting to be. A lot of strange things . . . I think one of the cast is . . ."

I could almost see her in the mirrored wall but not quite, just a subtle shape in the darkness, an occasional movement of black on black as she tried to get her thoughts together

I sighed and asked her, "Why the big mystery, kid? Just lay it out for me. What's the problem?"

"Well it's very delicate," she replied slowly, as though tasting her words carefully before letting them out. "And a lot is at stake. They're talking about keeping the cast together and taking this show on the road. A major booking agent is interested and the rumor is that several investors have come forward, so . . ."

"So what's the problem?"

"Look, a chance like this comes once in a lifetime. It's very important. To me and to a lot of other people."

"So I still don't—"

"I think someone is trying to kill our star."

"Come on."

"No, really, a lot of stange things have been happening."

I sighed again as I silently cussed myself for being lured out in the middle of the night by a theatrical imagination. "I get five hundred a day plus expenses," I said heavily. "So how much of my time can you afford?"

She slid a long white envelope over my shoulder as she replied, "We took up a collection. There's a thousand dollars here. We'll get more as we need it."

I turned around at that point, struck my lighter and peered at her in the flickering light as I asked, "Why all the mystery?"

She was trying to cover up, leaning back from the flame of the lighter with both hands at her face, in obvious alarm and suddenly very angry. "Put that out!"

I had only a glimpse, a brief impression of dark beauty and flashing eyes, before she knocked the lighter from my hand and ran out.

I was cussing out loud as I found the lighter and lit it again. The envelope was lying on my table and, yeah, ten one-hundred dollar bills were inside it.

I should have walked away and left it there but I wasn't sure she'd be back and I didn't want a wasted collection from hardworking kids on my conscience so I put it in my pocket and retraced my steps through the maze to the outside door, intending to return the money at the next performance of *La Mancha.*

Someone trying to kill their star! It's a tough business, I knew that, and I could understand the anxieties when that "once in a lifetime" break seems to be materializing, but I also knew that kids like these sometimes become so steeped in drama that they can lose touch with the real world—and I just wasn't buying the melodrama.

But then I stepped outside and instantly changed my mind about all that.

A gun boomed from somewhere among the parked cars and a bullet plowed into the bricks beside my head. I reacted instinctively, diving for cover behind the low wall of a walkway and staying as flat as I could get while five more sizzling rounds powdered the cement above me, all entirely too close for any kind of comfort. An engine kicked somewhere out there and a car tore away on screaming rubber while I was still cowering in the dust.

There was no thought of pursuit. I don't routinely wear a gun and I didn't even have one in my car.

I was just glad to be alive and still healthy.

Totally in the dark, sure, but reaching toward the light with all the brain I had left.

It was to be a damned long and painful reach . . . through melodrama to end all melodrama . . . and through a darkness unlike any I'd ever known. My name is Joe Copp. I've already heard all the wise remarks about the name, so spare me. I have been a cop of one kind or another all my adult lifetime and I'm crowding forty. I should have learned by now, you're saying, how to do it right and stay out of trouble. Maybe so, but I guess I never had that as my first priority. As a result, I bounced around a lot, one detail to another, one force to another—maybe trying to find superiors who'd be willing to let me do the job my way. Never did, so recently I've been my own boss, a private businessman, Copp for Hire—but not that much has changed, I still have a tough time doing it my way.

Like this case.

Don Pendleton

It started in the dark and damn near ended there. Pull up a chair, if you have a minute, and I'll tell you about it. Ever dream the impossible dream, like the man from La Mancha? Ever hold one in your trembling hands and *know* that it's suddenly becoming very possible? Ever willing to *kill* for it?

Some people are.

Oh yeah. Some people would kill for that dream.

CHAPTER 2

THE LOCAL COPS were on the scene that night almost before I could brush the powdered cement off my clothing. I played it dumb and told them nothing about the mysterious meeting in the hotel lounge, told 'em I thought maybe I'd surprised kids trying to pilfer from the parked cars and they bought the story for the moment. Still, that took some time so it was nearly five o'clock before I got home. I keep an office in my bedroom and the big bed was very inviting but I paused beside the answering machine as a conditioned reflex that can't be avoided any time I've been away

There were two new messages, recorded about twenty minutes apart. The first was from a Minnesota area code and urgently requested that I call back at the earliest moment, no name given. The other message was delivered in the whispery voice I'd already heard twice before, and all it said was: "Sorry for the quick exit but you forced it I'm glad you didn't get shot. Get to work but be very careful and please be discreet. I'll call again tonight."

I went to the bathroom and brushed my teeth, wondering about the strange-quotient of the night's events. If the gunplay had been merely a ploy to guarantee my interest, then the player was either a hell of a good pistol shot with a lot of self-confidence or a hopeless asshole who got lucky and didn't kill anyone with his dumb game. All six shots had been no more than an inch off the target. On the other hand . . . and what about the second dumb phone call? What was I supposed to get to work *on*?—and how more indiscreet can you get than six pistol shots in a theater parking lot at three A.M.?

I undressed and sat on the bed to return the call from Minnesota. I got an answer on the first ring from an older masculine voice with a definite midwestern sound to it. "This is Roger Johansen. Thank you for calling, Mr. Copp."

I casually inquired, "How'd you know it was me?"

An embarrassed little laugh preceded the explanation. "This is a pay phone. Didn't want my wife to hear any of this and get her hopes up again for nothing."

"Hopes for what?" I asked, wondering how long the guy had been prepared to stand at a public phone and wait for a call from a stranger two thousand miles away.

"Our son has been missing for more than six months now. Not a word from him and we've had no idea where he is. I had a call last night from California, a very mysterious call that sounded like one of these computerized voices. I was told that my son is in Southern California and that you could find him for me. Do you know anything about that?"

He sounded like a decent man. I sighed as I told him, "There are ten thousand missing kids from the midwest in Southern California today, Mr. Johansen, and another ten thousand will be arriving shortly. I don't know how you got my name but I don't do that kind of work."

"Then you are not the one who called me?"

"Absolutely not," I said.

"Well, this is very puzzling. I hope it is not just another cruel hoax. The inference was that you already know something about my son and perhaps could put me in touch with him."

I said, "Sorry."

"I don't understand the mentality of anyone who would do something like this."

"Me either," I assured him—then I had a second thought. "How old is your son, Mr. Johansen?"

"He's barely twenty-one. Dropped out of school in Chicago earlier this year and simply vanished. We haven't heard a word."

"Were you estranged before that?"

"Somewhat, yes. I've been paying for a degree in chemical engineering. We found out at the beginning of his senior year that he's actually majoring—or *was*—in theater arts. Things became a bit sticky after that."

To myself I said, "Uh oh."

To the worried father I said, "Send me a package, Mr. Johansen." I gave him the address and asked for recent photographs, names and addresses of known friends, a personality profile and any other items he could quickly lay hands on. "Send it by overnight mail," I added.

"Then you do know something."

"I might. Might not. But it's worth a shot to me if it's worth a hundred an hour plus expenses to you. Send me a five hundred dollar retainer and I'll bill you for the rest."

"I'm not a rich man, Mr. Copp. How much will this cost?"

"That will be up to you," I told him. "I'll report daily and you can tell me when to stop."

"I understand. And I'll get the package off to you right away"

I put the phone down and immediately rolled between the sheets. There was probably no connection between the man in Minnesota and a whispery voice in the dark, I told my waning consciousness, and I wouldn't charge the man or fan false hopes unless a connection did develop very quickly

On the other hand . . .

I went to sleep on that other hand, and I must have been very deeply asleep because it seemed like no more than an instant later—though the bedside clock was showing a few minutes past eight—when a very insistent finger on the back doorbell rousted me. I grabbed a towel from the bathroom and cinched it about my waist, then staggered to the door and opened it.

Two guys flashing federal credentials pushed inside and closed the door.

I said, "Shit!" and staggered on to the kitchen to put the coffee pot on.

I've had enough experience with feds to know that they are never quick to leave. I think they're all frustrated lawyers because they love to talk like they're examining a hostile witness in court, and they love to catch you in a lie before they get to the point of the examination.

So I put the damn coffee on and settled in as comfortably as possible dressed in a damp towel.

Meanwhile one of the feds is regarding me with a blank stare from the doorway and I guess the other is looking about the house—for what I really didn't care.

I'd placed three coffee cups on the table and pulled out a couple of chairs in an inviting fashion. They both joined me at the table a couple of minutes before the coffee was ready. We just sat there and looked at each other—both sides, I guess, waiting for the other to speak first.

Hell, I'd played those dumb games myself. I could wait. I did, until I poured the coffee, then I told them, "It's on the house."

These two guys looked like twin brothers. Dressed alike, combed their hair alike, even wore the same expression on their faces. The one to my left said, "Thanks, I really need this."

The one on my right winked at me and sampled his coffee with cautious lips. I winked back and poured down half a cup just for show and tried to hold back the tears as it scalded my throat clear to the esophagus.

"You're a tough guy, Joseph Copp," said Left with a little smile.

I shrugged and tested the voice with a weak, "It's a tough business."

Right chuckled softly and said, "I though P.I.'s hid in closets and snapped pictures of cheating wives."

I chuckled too and replied, "You think that's not tough?"

Left said, "He's not that kind of P.I. Are you, Joe?"

"Whatever pays the bills," I replied pleasantly, lying in my teeth. I do not do divorce cases, I do not do insurance cases, I do not do missing kids or irresponsible fathers or any kind of civil court stuff. I usually do what I damn well choose to do, and sometimes the bills don't get paid.

"What's paying your bills these days?" asked Right.

"Maybe I'm paid up a couple months ahead. Maybe I'm on vacation. Maybe you've got no right to ask. Did you show me your search warrant? I don't recall asking you guys inside."

"He's right," Left said chidingly to the other. "You can't ask a man in Joe's position to violate the sacred trust of his clients." He took a pull at his coffee. "Not even if it's going to save him a whole lot of trouble."

"Not even if it loses him his license," agreed the other in mock serious tones.

These guys weren't acting like any FBI people I ever knew. I told them, "I think I forgot to look closely at your credentials. Could I see them again, please."

Left smiled and stood up, went to the door, called back over his shoulder to the other, "Show the man your credentials, Larry."

I saw it coming out of right field but not soon enough to evade it, a haymaker with a pistol held flat in the palm of the hand. It crashed into the side of my head and sent me rolling across the floor. I would probably still be rolling if the wall hadn't been there, and I couldn't see very well with all those fireworks blazing through my skull but I heard Mr. Right okay as he bid adieu.

"Get smart for once in your life, Joe. Stay out of things that don't concern you."

His ass I would.

I knew now that I had myself a case.

So did those guys, and I was going to be all over their case . . . if I could just get my feet under me once again.

They were feds, all right.

But not FBI.

Those guys were deputy United States marshals, and I knew it even before I passed out, the briefly-flashed and quickly-glimpsed credentials flaring up out of the memory and leading me into beddie-bye.

This time I dreamed, and it wasn't of Jeannie. It was a

make-work dream, one of those problem-solving exercises that the right brain loves to frustrate us with, and it made no more damn sense than anything else that night.

But even in the darkness of the dream I knew that I had myself a red meat case. And I was going to eat some, if I could just find my feet again.

CHAPTER 3

I WOKE UP the second time that morning in my own bed again with a headache to end them all and dried blood in my nostrils, a naked woman lying beside me. She was very pretty but a total stranger and it took a moment for me to clear the fuzzies from my head and comprehend the situation. Not that I've never awakened beside a strange woman but this one's wrists were handcuffed to her ankles—picture that, if you can, left wrist to left ankle and ditto the other side for a highly vulnerable configuration—and her mouth was taped, eyes bulging in terror. The sweet-sickening odor of chloroform hung faintly in the air and someone was trying to break down my back door, which opens directly into the bedroom.

I was trying to assure my uninvited bed partner that things were not as they seemed when the door gave and two uniformed county cops entered with guns drawn.

So what the hell. It was a setup, sure, but how was I going to convince anyone of that? Those bastards had gone out and snatched a woman off the street somewhere, chloroformed her and put her in my bed trussed for Sadian delights while I snoozed under a light concussion, then tipped the cops.

They'd even used my handcuffs and the victim had not seen her abductors. She'd been grabbed from behind and knew nothing else until she awoke in my bed.

I was booked on charges of kidnap, assault and attempted rape and it was late that night before my lawyer could spring me. By then it was too late and I was feeling too sick to do anything else so I went home, repaired my door, and went to bed. Didn't even check my answering machine. I hadn't eaten anything all day—didn't feel like I could—and I'll have to say that I felt something like a whipped dog.

But don't get me wrong. Someone had shown me their power, sure, and I had to respect it. I am not, after all, Don Quixote so had never felt tempted to go out and fight with dragons. Didn't even have any impossible dreams. I guess what I am is a realist. But this thing had become intensely personal. I was no longer casually curious about the people in *La Mancha*, I was now ragingly curious about the march of intrigue that had seen me shot at, bullied by federal officers, then setup on very serious criminal charges.

Beside being a realist I am also a pretty well trained cop. I knew that I could not allow myself to start thinking like a victim. What had happened to me was purely incidental to whatever else was going down. I had to become the cop in the case. Hell, I *had* to. Otherwise I was just another victim, and victimhood is not a comfortable state with me.

So I wasn't giving up anything.

When I went home and took to my bed that night, I was actually girding for war.

And it's a good thing I slept well because I would not be doing it again until the war was over.

Strange thing about police work, even private work—you can go for months in the most boring routine imaginable, then suddenly the job can explode all over you without warning and you find yourself barely able to keep pace with it. In a matter of—what?—eight hours or so?—I had gone from yawning routine to battered jeopardy and still not even understanding what for. And I was still in the dark after another twelve to fourteen hours of humiliating and dehumanizing "legal process" which certainly had been designed to encourage me to remain in the dark forever where this case was concerned.

What case?

See?—it was even that dark. I didn't know what the hell was going down. It was fairly obvious, though, that it was very important to someone. Important enough, for sure, for someone to go to a lot of trouble to keep me out of it.

So the next morning I used my private little jiffy printing press to make a business card identifying me as a representative of Actors Equity Association and I paid an official visit to the East Foothills Dinner Theater to check their equity waiver status. The waiver is a special dispensation to small theater groups allowing them to pay less than scale.

I discovered that although the theater occupies hotel property it is independently managed by another group, none of whom were present at that time of the morning. The office wasn't even open but I found a beautiful gal in one of the back rooms who introduced herself as the director of the current play. She could not have been older than thirty and had the lithe, graceful body of a professional dancer, dark eyes that flashed with warmth and intelligence, and a very winning smile. Her name, she said, was Judith White.

My bogus card produced a soft frown, however, and an impatient toss of the pretty head as she complained, "Isn't twice in one month something like harassment?"

I frowned back and muttered something apologetic about overlapping responsibilities. "I'd just like a quick scan of your players," I added, "then I'll be on my way."

"This could all be moot in a few days anyway," she said, still resisting. "A new producer is coming in to package this show for a national tour."

"You're not closing the theater."

"Oh no, of course not. We're casting the next show right now." She glanced at her watch. "Well, in about ten minutes the tryouts start. You've really caught me at a bad time."

I said, "Just show me the file and I'll be out of your hair in five minutes."

She did even better than that. She handed me a bulging expando file, murmured "Excuse me" and left me standing there with it while she went on stage to greet a few early arrivals. The expando was labeled *Man of La Mancha—Cast File* and contained a sheaf of resumes complete with photos.

I didn't go through it there, just took it down the street to a *QuikPrint* and copied it on a self-serve machine. I was gone no more than fifteen minutes, left the file on her desk and let myself out again. Meanwhile the theater had filled up with hopefuls and the beautiful lady director was totally absorbed in casting the next play, probably wouldn't even remember that I'd been there.

I didn't know what I was looking for, you understand, didn't know that I would recognize it if I saw it. But you have to begin an investigation somewhere. I figured this was as good a place as any, in the dark, so I took the copied file home for a close study.

I'd forgotten entirely about the man in Minnesota so I was a little surprised to find the Federal Express package at my door. I scooped it up and took it inside but it was not very high on my list of priorities at the moment so I just dropped it on my desk for a later look.

What I was hoping to find, very quickly, was the identity of my mysterious "client" in the La Mancha case. She'd said "we took up a collection" which would mean, it would seem, that I had more than one client—but the whisperer was my contact and I wanted a look at the entire cast on the off-chance that I would find something familiar or recognizable before another contact. There had been two more messages waiting for me when I returned home from jail the night before. I knew that because I had checked the machine before leaving home that morning and decided to listen to them later; a third had been recorded while I was out gathering the cast file.

I studied the file for an hour and a half—it's a big cast—memorizing names and connecting them to career histories and photographs, then I listened to the messages.

One was from Minnesota. The package was on the way. Hooray.

The other two were from the whisperer.

One said, "When are you going to get to work? I expected to see you in the audience tonight." That's all.

The other, recorded at nine o'clock that morning, which is about the time I invaded La Mancha, said: "It's too late. They're playing for keeps. Forget it. Keep the money. Good luck to you."

Good luck, yeah.

I'm up for kidnap and attempted rape, so forget it and good luck.

I opened the package from Minnesota.

Didn't recognize the name, but the photo was sure familiar. I'd just memorized that face from the cast file—darker hair, darker skin, but all the planes and angles were the same.

"Someone is trying to kill our star," the whisperer had said to me in the darkened lounge.

The folks in Minnesota would be very worried to hear that.

I still had at least one client, it seemed, and I figured it was time for me to meet the man of La Mancha.

CHAPTER 4

AT FIRST GLANCE he appeared to be a man in his sixties with white hair and goatee, comically dressed in knickers and knee-socks, floppy vest and rumpled shirt, but of course he was costumed as Don Quixote, the improbable knight with the impossible dream, and that first glance was very deceiving. Behind the grease paint and false whispers stood an imposing figure of handsome virility no more than twenty-five years of age with sparkling eyes and genial disposition.

The players were getting ready for their matinee performance, chattering and clowning around with each other as they applied make-up and warmed up their voices. Very young, all of them. A couple looked like high school kids but I knew better. This was professional theater, don't misunderstand, primarily distinguished from Broadway by the amount of money invested in the productions and the lack of big-name talent, not the lack of talent itself.

The star and I shook hands in self-introduction and moved to a quiet corner of the busy dressing room, which was shared by all the male members of the cast, as I asked him, "Does my name mean anything to you?"

The voice was warm and his manner entirely open as he replied, "I'm sorry, no, I'm afraid it doesn't. Should it?"

I handed him one of my legitimate business cards and said, "Maybe not, but I've been hired to save your life."

The eyes narrowed just a bit at that and stayed that way as they examined my card but otherwise his manner remained the same. "Thanks, no offense intended, but my life is going pretty well right now."

"You know nothing about threats or attempts to kill you?"

The man of La Mancha chuckled and said, "Someone has played a practical joke on you."

"It cost them a thousand bucks," I told him soberly and produced the envelope with the money. "I came to return this. Who do I give it to?"

It was hard to ruffle this guy. He just grinned and said, "You can give it to me if you'd like but I don't know anything about it."

"Maybe someone else in the cast," I suggested.

He turned to regard the confusion of the dressing room, then looked at me with a sort of pitying grin. "There's not a thousand dollars between them," he said. "We work for carfare, not limousines."

I said, "Maybe it's a confusion of identities. Are you from Minnesota?"

The eyes gave a telltale little twitch. "No. I'm from Wisconsin."

"Close enough," I said. "Were you at the University of Chicago until a few months ago?"

Another twitch. "I studied in New York. You have the wrong man."

I returned the money to my coat pocket. "Guess you're

right. Sorry to bother you. Uh . . . but why don't you call home, Al. All is forgiven and they worry about you."

No more twitches. He just stared at me in silence. I nodded my head in farewell and went out.

The man from La Mancha was Alfred Johansen, no doubt about it. He was on the bill for La Mancha as Craig Maan.

And his twitches knew more than his mouth did.

I swiped a cast photo from the lobby and took it away with me, went straight to the post office and express mailed it to Minnesota, then went downtown to the FBI building for a talk with an old pal who shall remain nameless here. We'd worked together on a kidnap case in San Francisco years back, became friends despite the natural hostility between our respective agencies, and had kept in touch over the years. Duc to a physical disability, he'd been confined to a desk in Los Angeles for several years working liaison with the local police departments in the area. We got together occasionally for a beer and Monday Night Football but that had been the extent of it and actually I hadn't seen him for about a year.

I asked him, "How's the ticker?" and he replied with a grin, "Not quite strong enough yet for the Rams versus the Forty-Niners."

We repaired to the agents' lounge and got some coffee, sat down across a small table and brought each other up to date on our personal doings, then I asked him, "What do federal marshals do these days?"

He smiled and replied, "Anybody they can. Why? You thinking of applying?"

I said, "Hell no. But there are a couple I'd like some words with. Bobsey twins, look alike, dress alike. One might be named Larry."

He sniffed and said, "Sounds like Dobbs and Harney. Don't mess with those guys, Joe."

"No?"

"Uh huh."

"That bad, eh?"

"Pure poison. Stay out of their way."

"Can't. Couple of nights ago they snatched a woman off her front porch, chloroformed her, stripped her, and left her manacled hand to foot in my bed. I happened to be in it too, unconscious from a blow to the head, when the sheriffs busted in. Now I'm up for kidnap and attempted rape."

My FBI pal carefully set his coffee down and quietly said with no surprise whatever in the voice, "Yeah, that's heavy. They could do something like that, sure. Point is, why would they?"

"That is exactly what I am trying to find out, pal."

He said, "Sit tight," and went out.

He was gone about ten minutes.

When he returned he poured fresh coffee for both of us, sat down heavily, told me, "Don't push it, Joe."

"I have to push it."

"No you don't. Case will never get to court. Your victim will recant as soon as the other issues are resolved and all charges will be dropped."

"What other issues?"

"Can't talk about that, Joe."

"But the charges will be dropped."
"Yeh."
"Does the victim know that?"
"Sure. She cooperated."
"You're saying there is no victim."
"That's right."
"Dobbs and Harney, eh?"
"I shouldn't have given you that. I'm asking you to drop it."
I said, "Okay, it's dropped. But make me feel better, huh."
He stared at me through a long silence then muttered, "It's a hot case. Politically sensitive. Feel better?"
"Not much better. Hit me again."
My friend sighed, toyed with his coffee, finally hit me another tiny lick. "Federal Witness Protection Program."
I started breathing again long enough to say, "Oh shit."
"What?"
"Maybe I bulled my way into the china closet."
"Not yet," he assured me. "But you were getting close."
I said, "Yeah but I've been busy since then. Sent a package to Minnesota today by overnight mail. If their program has anything to do with Don Quixote, they'd better move their man fast."
"Don who?"
"Quixote, the man of La Mancha. It's a play at a dinner theater out my way."
"Oh that."
"That, yeah. Tell 'em. I'll be home in an hour. Tell 'em to come see me. But this time they shouldn't bare their fangs, I might kick 'em out."
I got up and walked out, left my man sitting there staring

at his coffee with a "what did I do?" look on his worried face.

By an act of congress, the federal government some years back began protecting prosecution witnesses who may be subject to retaliation by bigtime defendants. Sometimes that means secluding the witness in a safe house while the heat is on and until the testimony can be given. Sometimes it means later giving the witness a new name and a new life in a new place, a life on the lam under constant jeopardy, especially in organized crime cases.

My friendly informant at the FBI had used the words "hot case" and "politically sensitive."

Yeah.

I was worried too.

CHAPTER 5

THEY WERE ALREADY waiting for me when I got home. Not Dobbs and Harney but two FBI agents. I pulled around them and into the garage. They sat in their car until I got out of mine, then met me at the front door of the house. Even if I hadn't been expecting the call I would have known what these guys were.

"Mr. Copp?"

"That's right."

They introduced themselves and gave me plenty of time to examine the credentials, then asked if they could talk to me inside.

Very respectful, see, and by the book. I enjoyed the contrast and made a mental note to mend my own sometimes brusque ways in the future.

They were Special Agents David Shenks and Melvin Osterman, very sharp. I read them right away as easy and friendly, felt comfortable with them.

We went straight back to my office and I tried to make them feel as comfortable with me. They declined an offer of refreshments, wanted to get right down to business.

So did I.

Shenks said, "We'd like you to understand right up front, Joe, that we are familiar with your excellent background in police work. We'd like this to be a friendly meeting between professionals."

I said, "Then let's call it that."

There followed a brief silence, then Osterman told me, "We've come to deliver a formal apology on behalf of the bureau. We simply do not work that way and we want you to understand that. The entire bureau is embarrassed over the matter."

I said, "I understand. So am I. But just so I'm clear on the matter we're discussing . . ."

"Your arrest on false charges," Shenks explained in a flat voice.

I said, "Okay."

"The entire incident has been erased from the record," Osterman said. "The Los Angeles Sheriff's Department has been fully apprised of the unfortunate circumstances. They are cooperating. The incident did not occur."

"That's nice," I said.

Shenks added, "You can bill the bureau for your time and inconvenience, any reasonable amount. Is that fair?"

I said, "Sounds fair, sure. How'd this happen so quick?"

The agents exchanged glances. Osterman took it. "Well, as soon as it was brought to our attention . . ."

Shenks: "Naturally the bureau moved quickly to correct the matter and set the record straight."

I said, "But I brought it to your attention less than an hour ago."

Shenks: "The action was under review before that."

I wanted to get it straight. "Before I yelled."

"Right."

"And you guys beat me back here."

"Actually we were already on the way."

"So you do know about my visit downtown today."

They exchanged glances again.

"That's right," said Osterman.

"But you haven't asked about Minnesota."

Another conference of eyes only, then Osterman replied, "We were already here when we got the call from downtown, Joe."

"They didn't mention Minnesota."

"No. Is it important?"

I shrugged. "Maybe. Maybe not." I took the Federal Express airbill off the envelope from Minnesota and handed it over. Those airbills show the name, address, and phone number of the sender. "I sent this guy a picture of the *La Mancha* cast."

Shenks: "La Mancha?"

"The play."

"Oh. Right."

"You guys don't know anything about that, do you."

Osterman explained: "It's a sensitive case, Joe. You know how that goes. Sometimes the left hand is not privileged to know what the right hand is doing."

"And you guys are on the left hand."

He smiled. "There are both left and right hand aspects of delicate cases like these. But we'll see that your information gets to the proper hand."

"That would be Dobbs and Harney?"

"We can't answer that," Shenks put in quietly.

Osterman quickly added, "But we do appreciate your cooperation, Joe. Are we all clear now?"

I said, "Let's make sure. What you came to tell me is that

Dobbs and Harney overreacted to my interest in the case and did something dumb which the bureau overrode when you got wind of it."

Another exchange of glances. "That's about it."

"So why didn't Dobbs and Harney themselves come to square it with me?"

Osterman: "That seemed inappropriate."

Shenks: "You might question their good faith."

I said, "Right, I might at that. I also might break their faces."

Nobody laughed.

I said, "But of course it's a politically sensitive case."

"Uh . . . yes," said Shenks.

"You guys want me to just send a bill and forget it."

"The bureau hopes that you will."

"And butt out."

Osterman showed a thin smile and replied, "As the responsibly professional thing to do, yes, that would be best for all concerned."

"Suppose I don't go along with that. I can still send my bill?"

Shenks chuckled and said to Osterman, "I think he misunderstood the message."

Osterman was not laughing. He looked at me soberly as he told me, "You have no choice in that, Joe. You will butt out."

"Or . . . ?"

"Or you haven't seen the beginning of inconvenience," said Osterman.

"It's like that, eh?"

"I'm afraid so, if you insist on making it like that."

I was beginning to revise my reading of these guys.

Proper, sure, and by the book. But cold as ice beneath that easy surface. I said, "So you're not really apologizing for anything. You're just trying to give me a graceful exit. You couldn't make it stick anyway—and you never intended to, did you. Your cowboys paid a woman to help them stage that little scene in my bed rather than dirty their hands with an actual kidnap. Or maybe they used one of their own undercover people. Either way, you'd never want to take that act into a courtroom, would you."

Osterman showed me a thin, cold smile. "What do you want, Joe?"

"Maybe I want a bouquet instead of a brickbat. And maybe also I just want to exercise my constitutional rights as a citizen and businessman."

The special agents looked at each other then stood up abruptly to leave. "It's all a matter of perception," Shenks said. "You've been offered a bouquet whether you know it or not."

"I could sue you all, you know," I mildly reminded them as I followed them to the front door.

Osterman looked back at me as he stepped outside. "Dead men don't sue, Joe," he said quietly.

I stood in the open doorway and watched them get into their car and drive away.

So I'd been warned.

Okay.

Respectful and by the book, I'd been warned. Somehow it was a lot more chilling that way.

CHAPTER 6

SEE, IT WAS a very untidy package with loose ends sticking out all around and more contradictory than resonant. You naturally try to draw some kind of scenario when you're in the dark and possessed of only a few hard facts, but the scenario that was presenting itself still made very little sense to me.

I could accept right off the top Dobbs and Harney as a hotshot team of marshals protecting an important witness in some past or pending sensitive federal case. U.S. Marshals and their deputies are primarily officers and instruments of the federal district court, the court of appeals, and what is now called the Court of International Trade. They are considered to be national police officers and they have all the statutory powers of any lawman anywhere. They can seize property, arrest without a warrant, take prisoners anywhere in their district and remand those prisoners to jailers on their own authority. What's more, they can take them out of jail the same way. But you don't hear much about the marshals. They cut a low profile in the legal processes of this nation—but they are there, always there, and they have awesome powers when you think about it. A recent law modernized them as the U.S. Marshals Service, a bureau under the attorney-general, with their own director appointed by the president, but they still operate as marshals of the federal courts.

I had thought that the FBI had primary responsibility for the witness protection program. But I could also see how the marshals could be involved. It is their primary role and mission to provide for the security and to obey, execute, and enforce all orders of the federal courts. That could cover a lot, and it could mean overlapping responsibilities with the FBI. So there could be some scrambling there.

But even taking that at face value, it was hard to reconcile the other facts. The most logical scenario gave me a mystery person under federal protection for some sensitive reason and with the marshals involved in it. Since I had blundered into it, and since life had become very harsh for me since my meeting with a prospective client from the dinner theater, then the logic pointed to someone involved in the theater as the mysterious protectee. Doesn't take a genius to get to that point.

But the scenario also would seem to fall apart at that point.

If you want to hide somebody, would you put them on a stage in public view?

I wouldn't.

Of course, I'm no genius. If you give the guy a new identity and a totally new history, if you change the way he looks just a bit, then further camouflage him behind greasepaint and artgum, then bury him in a small community theater at the edge of a sprawling metropolis . . . well okay, maybe that would make some sense. Maybe he'd be as safe from detection there as anywhere.

Of course, though . . . if the guy turned out to have a really splendid talent, and the show began drawing attention from outside that small community, and if people started coming forward with offers to take that show on the road as a major production—could sudden fame be far behind? How safe then?

So maybe the package was not as sloppy as it seemed. Maybe . . .

Well look at it this way. The protectee is the one who made this show sensational enough to attract investors. Now he's in a quandry. It's a once in a lifetime opportunity. If he quits the show and looks for somewhere else to hide, will the moment ever come again?

Suppose he can't turn away from that opportunity. Maybe he even feels an obligation to the other players. If he walks away, so will the investors. More than one impossible dream would be smashed. So he cannot turn away. He calls his official watchdogs and tells them of his decision.

Now they panic.

Why?

Because they still want something from this guy. They need him for something hot, politically sensitive. Maybe a federal court has *ordered* that this crucial witness be given full protection and produced at some future date. "Produced" could be a key word there, where Dobbs and Harney were concerned. But they can't budge the kid's decision to jeopardize all that.

So what now? Try to scare him back into line? Give him

a little taste of mortality?—a little fear?—a reason to think again?

I could easily see Dobbs and Harney as cowboys, like U.S. Marshals of the old wild west, virtually autonomous and committed to their job.

Wouldn't be too hard to engineer a few suspicious "accidents" that are near misses. Shake the guy up. Make him come running back for protection.

Something like that could work, sure.

As a scenario, okay—marginally okay. The package is not so sloppy now.

Until someone else gets worried.

Someone who wants to tour the nation with a hit show, maybe several someones.

So then enter Joe Copp, onto a scene that is already under the watchful eyes of the cowboys. Maybe the whisperer's phone was under a federal tap. Maybe they had me coming in and were resolved to guide me through a revolving door and right back outside again.

That could explain the gunshots in the parking lot and the follow-up visit at my home. They didn't like the sound of me there so took the discouragement a step farther and tried to give me something more important to think about.

Stretched just a wee far, it could also explain the telephone call from Minnesota. A diversion, maybe, designed to suck me away into some quick and false resolution that would pad my wallet and satisfy my curiosity.

But they went too far, and that worried someone higher up or caused discomfort at the overlap. In that connection, I had to think that Shenks and Osterman had been dispatched *after* my visit to the FBI, although of course it was possible that they'd been telling the truth and it was just a coincidence that I'd already gone in on my own.

Whatever, the FBI was definitely interested and no doubt strongly involved—but what did that tell me?

And what if the Minnesota angle had not been engineered by the watchdogs themselves? Who turned Roger Johansen onto me? What if there is no Roger Johansen?

I talked to one, sure, but so far he is just a voice on a long-distance telephone connection, and I had only his word that the man in the photograph he sent me was his son Alfred.

So maybe "Roger Johansen" is a hit man looking for another kind of connection.

But how'd he get to me?

I had to skull this thing. Had to bring the loose ends together. I was like a blind man tapping his way through the darkness and it was driving me nuts. That is why I went back to the dinner theater. I had to know, see. I simply had to know. Then maybe I could make an intelligent decison about what I wanted to do with it.

Man of La Mancha is only very loosely adapted from the Cervantes novel, *Don Quixote*. Actually it's sort of a twist on Cervantes himself who has been thrown in prison during the Spanish Inquisition and he tells the Quixote story to his fellow prisoners to entertain and uplift them. So the title role is a mixture of both Cervantes and the fictional Quixote as the author becomes the character in acting out the story.

It's, you know, a bit fanciful but damned good theater. The entire play takes place in this Spanish prison. Most of the characters are male and they're all dressed in rags except the lead who, by some device, has this old theatrical trunk packed with costumes which he wears at various points in the story. There are only three female roles identified in the playbook I saw, which would seem to narrow the field of possible whisperers if mine had told the truth, but this particular production also used an offstage chorus to help Cervantes musically with his story, and there were four women in that group.

As I think I mentioned earlier, I'd already seen this production at this theater a couple of months earlier—but I wanted to see it again, now, from the top and with directed attention upon the players individually and the way they interacted with one another. You can learn a lot that way, by just watching people and checking interactions.

I didn't pay, this time. It's a thirty dollar tab with dinner and I did not want to be confined to a table anyway. The theater is set up Las Vegas style with none of the seats actually facing the stage, unless you can snare one of the VIP booths at the rear. This one is particularly nice, strictly class, with waiters in tuxedos and excellent food, probably holds several hundred people, has a large stage with curtains and all like any regular theater, not one of those intimate "in the round" setups.

I showed my badge at the maître d' podium out front and told the guy the absolute truth to get inside without paying. Most people never look closely at a badge, I don't know why unless the symbol is just so confronting and they're immediately impressed by it. It flustered the guy at the podium. I laid it out there for him to look at but his eyes bounced away instantly. I told him, "I need to just stand at the rear and observe for awhile. You understand. I'll be as unobtrusive as possible."

He even brought a stool and offered me coffee but I turned both down. "Are you investigating the accidents?" he whispered.

I just gave him a knowing look. He winked and went on about his business.

They serve dinner before the show and usually dessert during intermission. The waiters and busboys were still clearing the dinner tables when I arrived, which was a few minutes past the scheduled curtain time, and the show had not begun. I could sense a lot of movement behind the curtain and a moment later it was announced that the title role would be played during this performance by Johnny Lunceford so I immediately went back to find out what was going on.

Chaos was going on, back there

Apparently the lead was not the only one who'd missed the curtain. Several others were missing also and Judith White was busily reassigning roles and moving people about. They got it together rather quickly, I thought. I watched from the wing until the curtain went up, then went on backstage for a word with the beautiful director.

She was beside herself.

I asked, "What's going on?"

She asked, "Who the hell are you?"

I replied, "You know who I am," and handed over the money envelope.

She said, "What the hell is this? Go away. How'd you get back here? We're trying to put on a show here, sir."

I asked, "Where's Craig?"

"If I knew, I'd kill him. Will you get away and leave me alone!" She flung the envelope at me. It hit my shoulder and spilled the big bills at our feet. "My God!" she squealed.

I was attracting a lot of attention. Angry looking people were moving toward me, and among them I spotted my old pals Dobbs and Harney. They wore tuxes like the waiters out front and they were bearing down on me with malice aforethought.

So I left the money where it lay and went out quickly across the other wing.

The house was full, the show was on, and everyone appeared to be having a great time. Didn't want to spoil any of that. I went on outside, lit a cigarette, and awaited the inevitable.

CHAPTER 7

I STAND SIX-THREE and tip the scales well beyond the two hundred mark, so I'm no lightweight in ordinary company. I was not in ordinary company this time, though. These two were no taller than me but they were big, just big all over, with probably not ten pounds of body fat between them.

"Dobbs and Harney, I presume," I said softly as they scowlingly approached me just outside the theater.

The one I'd heard called Larry threw the first and only punch. I went under it and held onto the arm, stepped into it and levered the elbow into my chest. He froze under the sudden pressure, knowing what could happen next. I told his partner, "Back off, or I'll hand you his forearm."

"Believe it, Jack!" Larry grunted.

The other guy held up both hands at shoulder level and took a step backward, chuckled coldly and said, "I'd say it's a mess either way. You let go, he'll kill you. You don't, I'll kill you."

"Let's just talk about it and not kill anybody," I suggested. "Maybe we have a common cause that needs to be explored first."

I released the guy and pushed him away in the same movement. He rubbed the elbow and turned a respectful eye on me, then said to the other, "Let's listen."

"Other way around," I corrected him. "I've already taken all the lumps I intend to take from you two. Maybe I can respect it if I know why, but not this way. So why don't you explain it to me. First, which is Dobbs and which is Harney?"

Larry grimaced and replied, "I'm Dobbs."

So the other was Jack Harney. He was carefully lighting a cigarette and coolly checking me out over the flame from his lighter. "Don't give this jerk too much comfort," he growled to his partner.

"No, I think, we should talk to him again," said Dobbs.

"Forget it," I warned, "if it's going to be no different than the first time. Don't you guys really think you're just a bit too much? Who the hell do you hope to impress with the tough guy act? Talk sense to me and I can talk sense back. But if all you want is a rumble, well okay, I can do that too."

"I think he can," Dobbs said ruefully.

The other one sighed, took a deep pull from his cigarette and fixed me with a cold stare. "Some guys are just congenital assholes," he growled.

I said, "Right, but I won't hold it against you if you won't hold it against me. Where's your witness?"

"What?"

"Don't tell me you're moonlighting as waiters because you need extra cash. Your witness. The understudy is doing the show tonight, or didn't you notice?"

Harney did not take murderous eyes off me but his next statement was obviously directed toward his partner.

"Take a look."

We stood there and measured each other with our eyes at ten paces while Dobbs ran back inside the theater. The next words were his as he danced back into view and called from the doorway: "He's right! It's Lunceford!"

Harney dropped his cigarette and stepped on it, said to me in a cold voice, "Later," and walked quickly back inside.

But I could not wait for later. I had already reaffirmed my earlier decision. I knew that I had to become the cop in the case.

I didn't know where else to go at the moment so I went back inside and watched the rest of the show from the back wall of the theatre. So far I'd apparently struck out twice in trying to return the retainer and still didn't know who I'd actually been talking with that night in the lounge. I was not getting any clues from the people on stage and there was no sign of Dobbs or Harney out front.

The maître d' brought me coffee during intermission and this time I accepted it. Patrons were milling around, trying to divide their time between fancy desserts and the rest rooms, lot of traffic back and forth past my position at the wall.

At some time during all that, someone slipped the now worn envelope into my coat pocket. I didn't discover it until just before the curtain opened. The ten one-hundred dollar bills had been gathered up and neatly re-enclosed. There was also a scrawled note from "Elaine" which read: "Meet me at the stage exit after the show."

The name *Elaine Suzanne* surfaced immediately from my earlier study of the cast file. Age twenty-four, graduate of UCLA school of drama, single, a background in half a dozen community theater productions in the L.A. area, now cast as Dulcinea, the object of Quixote's affection. I watched her closely during the balance of the play, a strikingly pretty woman with long black hair and dancing eyes, and now and then I did pick up a head movement, a gesture that could tie her to my whisperer, though nothing whatever in the voice. Of course, these people were trained in voices and could probably sound like most anything a role may require.

As it turned out, she denied that she was the one when we met after the show. "We spotted you from the stage," she explained. "Judith thinks you're a nut. She insisted that someone return your money. I volunteered."

"Why?"

"Because I know you're not a nut. And we don't want you to give back the retainer. We want you to earn it."

"By doing what?"

"By seeing that nothing happens to Craig Maan. We thought you understood that."

"Who is 'we'?"

She gave me a riveting flash of eyes as she replied, "Some of the kids in the cast. We think it's a good investment."

"Why all the hokey pokey? Why didn't you simply come to me and lay it out in a businesslike way instead of whispering in my ear in the dark?"

"Because—no, you have it wrong, that wasn't me. Look, I chipped in and went along with the idea but I'm not the one who hired you."

"Who is?"

"I can't tell you that."

"Can't? Or won't."

"Both," she replied, raking me with those eyes. She seemed to realize just at that moment that we were walking through the parking lot. She planted her feet suddenly and asked me, "Where are we going?"

"To my car," I suggested.

"No you don't," she said firmly. "I had nothing like this in mind."

"What did you have in mind?"

"I just wanted to keep you on the job."

"I'm a bit confused," I told her. "I've already been fired. That's why I returned the fee."

"I know, but that was before we got together and took a vote. We overrode that earlier decision."

"What made you change your minds?"

She said, "Because we got a commitment from Craig."

"You did?"

"Yes. He wasn't involved, at first. Now he is. And he says let's go for it."

"So where is Craig now?"

"Nobody knows," she said worriedly. "He came in tonight and got ready, then walked out a couple of minutes before the curtain. Some of the guys went with him, but I don't know where or why."

"How many guys went with him?"

"Three, all majors. I mean, it could have wiped us out. But Judith put it back together and I think we did all right. That's why she was so rude to you backstage. She was under a lot of stress."

I asked, "Is Judith in on this?"

"I can't talk about that. It's a secret pact. So please don't—"

"Why all the secrecy?"

"It could seem self-serving, couldn't it."

I said, "Nothing wrong with that, kid. Especially now that Craig himself has joined you. Why would you suppose that someone wants him dead?"

She looked around to make sure we were alone, then leaned closer to quietly tell me, "This is absolutely confidential, top secret, you must keep it to yourself. Craig is an undercover cop. A narc. Maan is not even his real name."

I said, "Aw, come on!"

"No, really, that's why all the hush-hush. There's a price on his head. That's why he didn't want to take the show out."

"Or that's the story he gave you," I suggested.

"Why would anyone lie about a thing like that? And who wouldn't want to be the star of a hit show, unless . . . ? He only did it part-time, but he was really committed to it."

"When did he tell you this?"

"Just today. Well, there had been hints before that. I mean, some things just didn't jell."

I took her arm and said, "Come on."

She went along toward my car, but definitely under protest. "Where are we going?"

"To find Craig."

"I'd really rather not."

"Me too," I said, "but I guess I have to. Unless you'd rather I just go home and forget it."

But I guess she didn't fully commit herself to it until I'd seated her in my car. I went around and slid in beside her, kicked the engine, and asked, "Okay, where to?"

She bit her lip and said, "I guess we should try my place first."

"Your place?"

She nodded her head in confirmation. "Craig is my husband."

I gave her a hard look and replied, "The resume for both of you says single."

"I know. We were secretly married a month ago."

"Why secretly?"

She turned fidgety eyes to me and said, "That's none of your business. But I expect you to respect it and not go blabbing it around, none of this."

Hell, I wouldn't blab it, none of it.

Didn't even believe it, not any of it.

But it was damned good theater, and I was hooked. Yeah, I was really hooked.

CHAPTER 8

IT WAS A small but nice garden apartment less than ten minutes from the theater, all units at ground level with parking just outside the door.

Enroute, Elaine seemed to warm up a bit and began telling me about a series of "incidents" involving Craig Maan which just seemed too "queer" to be accidents. The trouble had begun two weeks earlier and just a few days after the investor group had come forward with their offer to produce the show for a national road company.

As she told me about it, a new scenario began forming in my mind—not the one she was painting for me but an alternate explanation of the events. In fact, if I had not already known about Dobbs and Harney and their interest in Craig Maan, I could have easily believed that the guy was a total phoney and spinning fanciful and self-aggrandizing stories to his friends for his own amusement. I have known people to do that, for no other reason than that it made them feel more important and interesting, if only to themselves.

"He was involved in two hit-run car accidents," she explained, "and he was shot at on the freeway. The police called it a random shooting. Can you believe that? Then his apartment caught fire while he was asleep in it and—"

"*His* apartment?" I interrupted. "Don't you two live together?"

"I told you our marriage is secret. Of course we don't live together. We talked about him moving in with me while his apartment is being reconditioned but then we decided it would be best if he just bunked around with the guys."

I said, "Did he bunk around with the guys for your honeymoon too, or is that also none of my business?"

"It's also none of your business."

"When was the fire?"

"Last weekend. Then on Tuesday, the day we all decided something had better be done to put a stop to all this, he was shot at again."

"Where?"

"In the parking lot outside the theater."

"So there would be witnesses to that."

"No. Craig had stayed behind to have a talk with the backers. He met them in the lounge after the show. Everybody had left the theater area by the time that was finished. I guess his car was the only one left over there at the time. So there were no witnesses. But the hotel security men heard the shot."

"Have you seen his apartment since the fire?"

"I have never seen his apartment."

I said, "Come on now, Elaine. You've been working opposite the guy for months, you say you married him, yet you've never seen his apartment?"

"I don't even know where he lives," she confided. "The address on his employment file is a fake."

"You checked that out?"

"Yes, I checked it out. I know what you're thinking, Joe, because I've thought it all myself. Craig has always been very mysterious about his personal life. I used to think he was just being theatrical or whatever, until today when he broke down and told us all about it."

"You're saying that you married the guy without knowing anything at all about him?"

"Well let's not talk about that, but yes I did. Leave it at that, please. Just find out who is behind all these attempts on his life, or at least try to keep him safe until we leave this area."

I said, "Do you know how nuts this all sounds? Have you been to the police?"

"No."

"Why not?"

"Craig would have come unglued. He told us about each of these incidents in the strictest confidence. We assumed that the police already knew about it. After all, I mean, he's a cop himself."

"Have you seen the damage to his car?"

"Yes."

"Bullet holes and all?"

"Yes."

"Any reason to wonder, at any time, if maybe Craig was just . . . you know, being dramatic?"

"Well yes, I already told you that I never knew whether to believe him or not, until just the past few days. He was always so mysterious and . . . well, sure, I wondered about it."

"So why, suddenly, are you buying everything?"

"Well . . . we saw you get shot at."

"You did?"

"We saw the bullet holes. And the pictures in the paper."

"What did Craig say about it?"

"It scared him bad. He thought they'd actually been after him—mistook you for him, I mean."

"So you told him the truth about me then."

"No. Not until today. He'd already made up his mind about the show. He'd decided to bow out. I think he'd made up his mind to just leave town very quietly. We didn't think it would serve any purpose to tell him about you, not until we saw you this afternoon before the matinee."

"Why did that change anything?"

"We had to tell him. He thought you were a hit man and he was going to run right then. So we told him. We thought he'd be mad about it, but he wasn't. He went out and checked on you. He has access to the police files, you see. And that reassured him very much. So much that he had a complete change of heart. When he came in tonight to dress for the show, he told me that he'd decided to stay and fight back. He wasn't going to let anyone stand in his way. Then thirty minutes later he walked out. So I don't know what . . . nobody knows, we're totally mystified."

"Did you see him walk out?"

"Sure, we all saw him."

"So he went under his own steam."

"I guess so. The other guys went after him. Nobody came back and it was curtain time. So . . ."

So, yeah.

We'd been sitting outside her apartment during the final half of that conversation.

We went inside then, and Elaine turned on the lights. Craig Maan was there, seated on the couch.

Waiting for us in the dark, you might say—still made up

for the stage but now totally naked and tightly bound hand and foot—but I guess he hadn't minded any of that for long.

His throat had been slashed from ear to ear, and he'd been dead for quite awhile.

I silently apologized for my alternate scenario, and for all the uncomplimentary things I'd been thinking about the guy.

A dream had ended there, yeah . . . and maybe a nightmare or two.

CHAPTER 9

SINCE THE CRIME scene was located in an unincorporated area of San Bernardino county, the police response was by the sheriff's department—and I happened to have a nodding acquaintance with the detective in charge of the initial investigation, guy named Art Lahey.

I took him aside and told him the circumstances as I understood them but cleaned up a bit for the sake of credibility, and suggested that he notify the FBI. I pointedly named special agents Shenks and Osterman, and Lahey took it all down.

Elaine was in a mild state of shock. She went that way at the first sight of the corpse and I had taken her back out to my car even before phoning in the find. Then I'd gone back inside to call it in and to look around on my own before the cops arrived. There was no sign of a struggle, no sign of forced entry, nothing apparently out of place or even disturbed. Except for the area around the couch, which was of course a bloody mess, the whole place was neat as a pin. There was only one bedroom and a small combo kitchen-dining-living room, tiny bathroom, but all very nice and feminine like an ad in Good Housekeeping.

She lived there alone, yeah, that much was obvious—no masculine articles of clothing or toiletries, nothing like that.

The responding patrolmen immediately evicted me to the front lawn and secured the scene with yellow tape, then we stood around and waited for the homicide response while I provided them with the data necessary for their patrol reports. I'd filled out several thousand such reports myself during a fifteen year police career, so I knew what they needed and that's all I gave them. The rest would keep for the detectives.

I was glad to see Lahey. Some of these guys can be real jerks sometimes but Art Lahey is a highly intelligent and coolheaded cop. We'd brushed official elbows a few times over the years and it had never been an unpleasant experience.

I went through the whole thing with him—all he needed to know at the moment, that is, including the angle on the U.S. Marshals—but to no great detail. It was obvious that Elaine Suzanne was in no condition to be questioned. I wanted to get her away from there, and I promised Lahey that I would produce her on demand. I pointed out that she had been virtually in my sight and on stage in front of hundreds of people throughout the evening, therefore she could not be a viable suspect.

He agreed and allowed me to take her away.

By then it was past midnight. I ran her by a friend of mine who practices medicine the old-fashioned way. She checked her out and gave me a few pills, told me to put her to bed and let her sleep it off. Elaine had said not a word to me since the discovery of the corpse in her living room, and I'd left her alone too, but she did talk a bit with the doctor—"I'm fine"—"I'll be okay"—"Thank you"—that sort of thing.

As we returned to my car, I asked her, "Where would you like to go?"

She replied in a monotone, "I don't know."

"Any family in the area?"

"Not anymore."

I sighed. "You can stay at my place tonight if you'd like."

"Okay," was all she said to that offer, and without any noticeable enthusiasm.

Don't know why I felt responsible for the kid, I just did. Well, she was sort of a client, I guess. A piece of an ex-client anyway. I still had the retainer. Dawned on me that I had failed. I shrugged it away. I'd never actually agreed to do anything, had been trying to return the money, had been jailed, fired, and sort of re-hired, but I'd never actually been given an opportunity to succeed or fail in anything. So why should I feel that I had failed anyone? I decided that I hadn't and that felt better, for a moment anyway.

I'd become involved in other lives, though, and it was never easy for me to insulate myself from people and their problems. Craig Maan, or whoever, was dead, sure, but the dead are never the problem. Death is the end of problems. It was fairly easy for me to let the dead go. My troubles were always with the living. I knew that, and I knew that I was opening myself to troubles but I couldn't just turn this kid out onto the street in the middle of the night and I knew damned well that she didn't want to go home even if she could, not with the dried blood of her dead "husband" dominating that small apartment.

So I took her to my place.

I live in an unincorporated area, too, but in L.A. county. Bought a house up in the hills overlooking the San Gabriel and Pomona valleys, did it at a great time before the development pressures became intense out that way, got it relatively cheap and now my equity is worth probably ten times what I have in the house. What's better, I'm not jammed in cheek to jowl with hordes of other people. I'm up there with the horsey set, and though I personally dislike horses myself—well, nothing against the horses, just their byproducts—the size and arrangement of the lots gives me privacy bordering on seclusion and there's plenty of room to stretch. My neighbors can't hear me peeing in my toilet—and not everybody in Southern California can say that. Best of all, I'm only a few minutes above every convenience our civilization can offer, so it's not like I'm isolated or deprived in any way. I even gave up my office space down below and moved it all into my bedroom since most of my business comes via telephone anyway and it's more comfortable at home, gives me more time for gardening and working in my woodshop.

Remind me to tell you sometime about my woodworking. Some day I may decide to make a living at it. Started as a hobby, something to keep me busy during slow times, but one thing led to another and I've done a few custom kitchens for hire and for some pretty good money. It's an option, if things get too ratty in police work or if I decide to take another bride. Marriage and police work don't mix well, I've found, at lest not for me and not for the women I've tried to mix into it.

Anyway, I took Elaine Suzanne to my castle in the hills with the intention of offering her the comfort of my rollaway which I keep on hand for such occasions. I only have one bedroom now, knocked out some walls and did some radical restructuring inside to give me plenty of stretch—hate being confined—and for at least a presumption of luxury. Nothing wrong with luxury. I recommend it to everyone, even the poor. I'm poor, but you'd never know it to look at my house, so most of the time I don't know that I'm poor.

You get to it along this little tree-lined lane, past half a dozen other "estates" as the realtors call them, and dead-ending in a circle at my place. Hardly anybody ever comes back there unless they're lost or looking for me, and I consider that ideal.

There are drawbacks, of course. The area is not well lighted at night unless I go in and turn on my own floods—and the way the lots are staggered along the hillside and mixed in with the old trees that have stood there most of this century, you can get a feeling of total isolation and vulnerability to attack if you have any reason to expect such a thing.

Don't know where my head was, but I guess I wasn't expecting anything like that when Elaine and I rolled in there at about one A.M.

I hit my garage-door opener at the usual twenty yards out and rolled on into the garage without a pause. It's attached but I have saws and lathes occupying the inner wall and blocking direct access to the house, so I have to go around to the front door to get inside.

No big deal, it's only about twenty paces out of the way, but it sure made things easy for the guy who was laying out there on the hillside waiting for me.

I heard the crack of the rifle and felt the big slug whistle past my nose as I rounded the corner of the garage with Elaine in tow. She'd taken a pill at the doctor's house and was sort of loosey-goosey halfway out of things and I was half-walking, half-dragging her toward the house when the attack came.

I took us both to the ground and rolled her ahead of me toward the doorway with bullets thwacking in all around us as the fusillade continued. I use the word fusillade advisedly; there were at least ten rounds, all from the same gun and obviously from a highpower rifle, maybe a thirty-thirty. I know it made a mess of my stucco and penetrated the garage wall to tear into my woodworking tools, I discovered that later.

But we got inside untouched. I carried Elaine through to the bedroom and dropped her on the bed, ordered her to stay there, then I grabbed some firepower of my own and went out the back way to see what I could see.

I saw nothing, but I heard a car tearing along the lane above me and knew that the shooter was beating a hasty retreat. So much for that, but I'd spotted the muzzle flashes and I wanted a close look at the point of attack, went on up there on foot and found some still-hot expended brass that had been ejected from a thirty-calibre breech, took them back to the house and hurried in to reassure my guest for the night.

Except that I had no guest for the night.

She wasn't there—not on the bed, not in the bathroom, not anywhere inside that house or staggering along the lane or running down the highway.

Elaine Suzanne was simply nowhere.

CHAPTER 10

I CALLED ART Lahey right away, felt an obligation to do that since I had taken responsibility for a major witness and now I had lost her. Took a few minutes to get him on the line. He was still at the murder scene; they had to radio a patrol unit and pass instructions for him to call my number. I made coffee while I was waiting for that, thought of all the things I could have done and should have done but hadn't done over the past few days.

It's a sheepish sort of feeling, a smarting and rankling in the pride of a man who has made police work his life yet now finds himself stumbling around blindly in the dark unable to find his ass with both hands. Wasn't humbling, it was maddening, and I was getting mad as hell under the descending conviction that I had been set up from the start and systematically lied to and misled throughout. A distinction is implied there. It's the difference between walking into a dark room and groping along the wall for the light switch or being lured into a dark room with no switches and the door locking behind you.

Where I was, at this point, was the sudden realization of that distinction.

Someone had set me up—but for what?—and why?

That's where I was at when Art Lahey returned my call.

He said, "Thanks for calling. I was about to get back to you anyway. Your identification of this victim is the only one we have. It doesn't check out at DMV and we haven't been able to contact the employer you gave us. The hotel people don't know anything about the theater people and we can't reach this Judith White, no phone listed. The FBI wouldn't give me anything. You'll have to bring the lady in, Joe. Right now."

I swallowed hard and told him, "That's why I called. I can't bring her in. I don't know what the hell is going on, pal, but I came home to an ambush and now your witness is missing. I believe she was snatched while I was responding to the ambush. That was just minutes ago."

There was strain in that voice as he asked, "Anybody hurt?"

"Not that I noticed. I was unarmed, couldn't return fire. It was a hillside sniper at about fifty yards out with a thirty-calibre rifle. The woman was sedated and barely able to walk. We were like ducks in a shooting gallery but we got inside the house untouched. I left her there, armed myself and responded but it was a shoot and run, guy was already gone. When I got back, so was your witness. She could hardly walk, Art, let alone run. Somebody took her. I think it was set up that way."

There were maybe ten seconds of silence before his response to that information, and I could hear cold suspicion in the voice when he did respond. "Maybe it was. Tell me. How was this so-called Craig Maan dressed the last time you saw him?"

I said, "Last time I saw him he was in costume for the

play but that was this afternoon. I told you that he walked off the stage this evening just minutes before the curtain was scheduled to go up, so I'd guess he was dressed the same way then. Sort of comical looking blue knickers, gray knee-socks, a floppy vest and a tattered shirt. Did you find that?"

"We found nothing in this apartment but women's clothing. Could this guy be a transvestite, Joe?"

I hadn't wondered about that myself. I told him so, adding, "He didn't live there, Art. Elaine Suzanne told me he'd been staying temporarily with friends. I told you that."

"Yeah, you told me that. But this thing has all the signs of a sex crime. Did Miss Suzanne tell you that she lives in that apartment?"

"You telling me she doesn't?"

"That's not the name on the rental agreement. And the manager doesn't remember what the tenant looks like, says she never sees anyone coming or going, the rent is paid by mail."

I said, "We've got a puzzler here, Art."

"Tell me about it. Have you reported your incident or is that what you're doing now?"

"No, it's L.A. county jurisdiction. Haven't called it in yet. Wanted you first. Thought maybe you'd like to be here to see for yourself while the evidence is hot." I gave him the address, although the patrolmen at the murder scene already had it, and I gave him directions.

He said, "Okay. That's not far."

"Ten minutes if you step on it."

"You'd better call it in, Joe."

"Soon as we hang up," I assured him.

But I waited five more minutes anyway. Didn't know

why, at the time, not at the front of the mind. But I guess I was starting to come in from the dark.

There had been many questions that I had been patiently waiting to ask of Elaine Suzanne. Like, why had she told me that ridiculous story about a "secret marriage" with Craig Maan when obviously they were not living together and she seemed to know very little about him. Why had she suggested that we begin our search for Craig at her apartment when by her own mouth she had no idea where he was staying and did not know why he had abandoned the play as he did—and, with this new information from Lahey, why had she rented the apartment under a different name, or had she?—was that really her apartment and did she actually live there?

Did she know Dobbs and Harney, as waiters or whatever, and did she know of the relationship between them and Craig?

Who were the "three other guys" who left the stage behind Craig that evening, and what had been their relationship with the murdered actor?

If, as she seemed to believe, Craig's death had been the act of vengeful drug dealers, why had he been stripped naked and bound hand and foot before being killed when there was no suggestion of torture or violent interrogation, no evidence of a struggle—and why had he been killed in her apartment?

There were more questions than that, of course, but I would have settled for the answers to those at the moment. I had thought that I would give her a chance to recover a bit from the shock before asking her anything, but certainly someone was going to ask about such things and

I preferred to be the first in line, if only to satisfy my own curiosity.

My thinking had changed, of course, following the ambush and Elaine's disappearance. Evidently more than my own curiosity had to be satisfied now. I was coming out of the dark and I did not like the view from the new perspective.

But all of that would have to wait now. I was clearly involved in a homicide and God knew what else. I'd found my ass. And it was not in a comfortable position.

They all got there at about the same time, moving like a caravan along my lonely little lane—L.A. county, San Bernardino county, the FBI—five cars in all, more than a dozen officers, and they had not come for tea.

The two FBI agents sort of stuck to themselves, listened and watched but never spoke to me directly and apparently took no active part in the investigation. I gathered that they'd come with Lahey.

There was not a friendly face in the pack, including Lahey's, and the FBI people I'd not seen before.

They took measurements and ran triangulations from the bullet holes in my wall, dug for slugs and emptied my garage looking for more, trampled several flower beds and paced off the distance to the spot on the hillside above the house, milled around up there and returned with bagged evidence, compared it with the brass I'd brought down myself, asked me the same questions over and over until I wanted to kill, and then they all departed—all but Lahey.

He still wasn't friendly, but we went to the kitchen and drank the coffee I'd made a couple of hours earlier.

"My ass is hanging out on this, Joe," he quietly told me over the coffee. "I should have taken the woman into custody. You know that."

"Know it now," I admitted. "At the time, it seemed okay."

"Why was she snatched, do you think?"

"Obviously someone didn't want her talking to us."

"Maybe. And maybe *she* didn't want to talk to us. Maybe she walked away on her own."

"How many times do we have to go through this?" I snapped. "I've said it fifty times, I wasn't gone more than a couple of minutes. Even if she'd been wide awake and functional, I could've chased her down. I tried, and I couldn't."

"That's bullshit and you know it. In this country she could have simply gone to ground anywhere, concealed herself and crept away after you quit looking. Let's talk about why she would do that."

I glared at him and said, "Okay, but I have to tell you that I'm growing damned sick of theorizing."

He grinned suddenly and said, "Ready to kick butt, eh?"

"Any but my own," I said. "And you should take that as advice for yourself. You acted properly. The woman was clearly in a state of shock."

"She's also an accomplished actress," he pointed out.

I waved the suggestion off. "There's a smokescreen over this whole thing but I don't think she was acting. Neither did the doctor. She sedated her, and the medicine had taken effect before we got here. Even with heavy slugs chewing up the wall all around her, she was totally helpless, unable to fend for herself. That would have broken the act, if that's what it was. It didn't. I had a hell of a time getting her inside and she was a rag doll when I dropped her on the bed. It wasn't an act."

Lahey nodded his head as though accepting the argument, but then he said, "But let's say that she could have roused herself and run away on her own. Why would she do that?"

"You tell me. Maybe it really wasn't her apartment, and maybe she led me there for reasons of her own, but I don't believe that she knew in advance what we were going to find there."

Lahey leaned back and gave me a calculating look. "Did she lead you there, Joe? Or did you lead her there?"

I said, "Don't get crazy."

He took an envelope from his inside jacket pocket, extracted a glossy polaroid photo and displayed it at his chest to give me a good view. "Look like anyone you know?" he asked coldly.

It was a very recent photo of me, a full figure frontal of Joe Copp, the would-be cop in the case. I was wearing a very surprised face but nothing else.

"Where'd you get that?" I asked him.

"We found it at the murder scene."

I looked at it again, and this time I recognized the background. I also remembered when the picture had been snapped. About two weeks earlier, as I was stepping out of a shower at my gym down on Foothill Boulevard. The flash of the camera had taken me by surprise, and I'd had only a glimpse of the guy who took it before he stepped out the door and disappeared. Hadn't tried to explain it to myself at the time, merely shrugged it away and hadn't thought of it since.

"I can explain that," I told the cop.

"I hope so," he said. "We found it beneath the sofa cushion. The man died while sitting on it, or else it was put there later. There was dried semen on his thighs and penis."

I experienced a suddenly plummeting stomach.

"That's what you meant by *sex crime*," I said weakly.

"What'd you do with his clothing, Joe? We couldn't find a scrap of it anywhere."

"You go get screwed, guy," I told him. "And do it in your own jurisdiction."

Lahey sighed, got to his feet and went to the door, turned back to say, "It's a viable theory. Enough that I think you shouldn't be playing games with us. If you know more than you've said, now's the time to bring it forward."

I knew that.

Yeah, I knew that.

But at the moment I had not a damned thing to bring forward into the light.

CHAPTER 11

IT WAS GETTING onto four A.M. when Lahey left my place. I tried to get in a quick nap but it was a fitful one and did nothing at all for my state of mind, was up at six for a shower and shave, a quick breakfast and an early start. I wanted to get to Judith White before the sheriffs could, hoping for any edge I could find. It was a Friday morning and traffic was light, not a lot of people stirring at that hour.

I had figured to break into the theater and find Judith's home address, but that wasn't necessary. The stage entrance was open and the lady was in her office amid stacks of resumes and photographs, hard at work at seven A.M.

I stepped quietly inside and watched her for a moment before making my presence known. The old adage about beauty and brains had no meaning here. Obviously this woman possessed both, honey-blonde hair clipped pertly close in soft curls to follow the contours of a perfectly shaped head, a generous mouth with soft lips and pearly teeth, eyes sparkling over some great inner adventure—but they sizzled when she looked up and saw me standing there.

I grinned soberly from the doorway and said, "Knock knock."

"Not again," she said despairingly.

I went on in and sat on the edge of a chair with my hands clasped on my knees, sort of like body language to let her know I didn't plan on getting too comfortable. "Sorry to bother you," I said solemnly.

She tossed her head and glanced meaningfully at the stacks of resumes cluttering her desk. "Why do people always say they're sorry but do it anyway? You were in here the other day, too, weren't you, posing as an equity inspector."

I said, "Uh huh," and produced my ID, handed it to her. "Look at it carefully," I suggested, "so you don't get the wrong idea about this visit. I'm private, not public. I'm in a hell of a mess and I need your help. Will you help me?"

She gave me a cool appraisal as she handed the ID back, seemed to be thinking about it, finally told me as she relaxed into her chair with a sigh: "Why not? I've got three whole days to cast this next show. How much of my time do you need, Mr. Copp?"

"Call me Joe," I requested, and relaxed a bit myself. "First I'm afraid I have some shocking news for you. Craig Maan was killed last night."

If there was a visible reaction there, I couldn't detect it in the first uptake. "How was he killed?"

"His throat was slashed."

The eyes moved a bit on that one. "Are you serious?"

"Yes, I'm entirely serious. Someone in your cast hired me several days ago to keep Craig alive. I didn't take it all that serious at the moment, and in fact last night I came in here to return the retainer."

"Why did you bring it to me?"

"Seemed as good a guess as any. I didn't know who to give it to because I didn't know who'd given it to me. I left here last night with Elaine Suzanne after she brought the thousand bucks back to me and asked me to stay on the case. We went looking for Craig, found him in an apartment up near Rancho Cucamonga. Elaine told me it was her apartment but it's not in her name. Craig had been dead for at least two hours. He was naked, tied hand and foot, throat cut from ear to ear. He—"

She surged to her feet and moved quickly to the door, paused there to look back and say, "Excuse me a second," and went on out.

I lit a cigarette and smoked it half way before she returned. I'm cutting down but it's hard to quit entirely, especially in stressful times. I was feeling plenty of stress.

Judith was carrying a tall glass of water when she came back in. She'd been crying but seemed fully in control again.

"I wanted to kill him myself last night," she quietly told me as she returned to her chair. "Who did it?"

I said, "Well, that's the big question of the moment. Another one is why. I'm hoping you can help me with the second one."

"Well, he was the biggest liar I've ever known," she said matter-of-factly. "And he was almost totally irresponsible. Other than that, though, the sweetest guy in the world. And a great talent. With the right break . . . what do you want me to tell you?"

"I'd like to know why someone would want to kill him, for real."

She had to excuse herself again. I waited, but not

patiently. Didn't know how much time I might have before the posse arrived. She came back after a minute or two with a blotchy face and said, "I'm sorry. Where were we?"

"Why was he killed." I made it a statement, not a question.

She shook her head. "I wouldn't have the faintest idea. Such a waste."

I said, "Yeah. There's a lot of waste in our world today. But tell me about Craig. What did he waste?"

"Time," she replied immediately. "And energy. Talked too much, maybe he dreamed too much. Lied too much."

"About what?"

"About everything. Many actors do that. It's sort of like . . . being unable to distinguish between the dream and the reality."

"Did he tell you that he was an undercover cop?"

She laughed softly. "No. But I wouldn't put it past him."

"Did he ever tell you that he was being guarded by federal marshals?"

She wrinkled her nose. "No. What is a federal marshal?"

"Something like a sheriff," I explained, "except at federal level. The two guys who were chasing me backstage last night, the two in waiter's garb—do you know those guys?"

She said, "They work here, sure."

"As waiters?"

"Yes."

"How long?"

"Waiters come and go," she replied. "I don't know how long they've been here."

"Had you ever noticed them in company with Craig?"

"No."

I told her, "Those two are deputy United States

Marshals. It's been hinted to me that they are protecting someone here, maybe Craig, under the Federal Witness Protection Program. Does that give you any quivers?"

She shook her head in negative response but the eyes were beginning to show some new wonderment.

I asked, "How well do you know Elaine Suzanne?"

"Not personally at all," Judith replied. "This is her first production with us."

"Talented?"

"Oh yes."

"More or less reliable?"

"More or less, yes."

"More than less?"

"Less than more," she said.

"Were she and Craig honeys?"

"I guess she'd like to be."

I saw something in the eyes there that prompted me to ask, "Was Craig gay?"

"How would I know?"

"Women are usually the first to know."

"I don't mix much with the cast offstage," she told me. "The actors come and go. I don't, I'm here all the time for all the shows—and while we're staging one play I'm usually trying to prepare for the next one."

"This one has had an unusually long run."

"Yes."

"What made this one special?"

"Craig made it special."

"He was that good?"

"He was the best I've ever seen in that role."

"So you weren't surprised when someone stepped forward to package it for the road."

Her eyes clouded. "Well . . . I'm wondering now . . . that could be another of Craig's tall tales."

I reached for another cigarette but didn't light it, just held it—that helps sometimes. "Why do you say that? You've never met the new producers?"

"No. But Craig pointed them out to me one night and—"

"You mean there was never any formal . . . ?"

"Nothing involving the theater, no. That would not be necessary. We don't own the play. We merely produce it under license from the owners. Anyone can do that. So I really wasn't involved in any of the talks and wouldn't have been unless and until the new producers wanted me to direct or stage-manage or whatever."

"So all you know about any of this came from Craig."

"That's right."

"You said he pointed out these people to you?"

Her eyes twitched. "Yes. That's why now I'm wondering, after what you've told me about Larry and Jack. You say they're federal agents. Craig told me they're the new backers."

"Working as waiters?"

"Craig has a way of making the ridiculous sound absolutely sane. These men always work that way, he said. They pose as ordinary people so they can be close to ordinary people and learn how ordinary people are reacting."

"They could sit comfortably in the audience and do that," I pointed out.

"Oh, but these men are also greatly interested in the way the cast works together and pulls together backstage and offstage."

"And you fell for that?"

"I really felt no need to challenge it," she replied.

"You're telling me that Larry and Jack, the waiters, are the backers who are going to put this show on the road?—and that only Craig had their ear?"

"That's about it," she said. "So one of you, either you or Craig, is a very cruel liar. And of course Craig would be the cruelest, if it's his lie. Because he's had these kids so high . . ."

I put my cigarette away and told her, "I think maybe you've given me what I came for."

"You mean . . . ?"

Yeah. That's what I meant. Maybe someone in that "so high" cast found out about the cruelest lie of all.

And maybe he or she or they got mad enough to kill.

CHAPTER 12

I HAD A whole new angle on the situation now and a lot to think about but I still was not sure that I had all I could get from Judith White. She was plenty sharp, had one of those blessed female minds that can cut straight through all the crap and trivia to instinctively seize and size an issue at its naked core. Also I was beginning to like this woman quite a bit.

So I talked her into walking over to the hotel coffee shop with me, primarily because I didn't want to be interrupted by the official police but also because I felt that a public atmosphere could help her to relax and open up a bit more.

On the way over I asked her, "Okay to call you Judy?"

"I prefer Judith," she replied—then added, with a little smile, "Except in intimate moments. I couldn't expect Cary Grant to say, 'Judith, Judith, Judith,' could I."

So Judith it was, for the moment—with maybe a hint of Judy in the future—but at least it was a start in the right direction. Over coffee and Danish I learned that she was older than she looked—thirty-two—and had once dreamed of starring on Broadway herself. She'd landed a role in a national touring company straight out of Pasadena

City College, had later toured Europe and Japan, then decided that was not the way she wished to spend the rest of her life.

"I gave it five years," she told me, "and during that time I saw too many middle-aged people, fine talents all, who'd given it their lives and everything else—home, family, even self-respect. I settled for less, and I believe in the end I will have more."

"And less is . . . ?"

"What I'm doing now. I still have the creative outlet, the fun, the excitement, but it's not burdened now with the dream."

"Dreams are important," I suggested.

"Reality dreams are important," she countered. "Most theater dreams are totally unreal, especially if they're all aimed toward Broadway. I try to tell the kids who come through here to relax and enjoy it—hey, people are paying to watch them perform. If you'd perform without pay—and you're no performer if you wouldn't—then hey, you've made it, you've arrived, enjoy it."

I guessed, "Craig couldn't do that."

"Well that's just it, that's what so sad, Craig *did* do that . . but to a fault. Craig seemed to live for that moment, that moment *on the stage* when the dream was working. Craig's problem, you see, was that he often could not or would not turn it off when the curtain came down."

"Give me an example."

"He was into American Indian mysticism—barely into it, I'd guess, Craig was no scholar. But he'd picked up this shamanistic idea that the dream time is the real life and the real life is the dream. He—"

"Sort of fits the *La Mancha* theme, doesn't it?"

"Pretty close, yes, pretty close. But the Indians still went out and hunted the buffalo and killed it and ate it because they knew that real or not they still had to feed themselves to keep the dreams alive. But you're right—I've often thought that Craig was so right for *La Mancha* because he was really playing himself up there on that stage."

I said, "*La Mancha* is a story within a story."

"It's a story within a story within a story," she corrected me. "And it's also a dream within a dream within a dream. The prisoner Cervantes is a defeated and dying old man who invents the fictional Alonso Quijana as an inept, ineffectual and perhaps demented old country gentleman who transforms himself into Quixote, an inept, ineffectual and certainly demented knight who sees the world exactly as he chooses to see it, all other evidence to the contrary—but then that illusion is seen as a transforming vision of human life as it ought to be, not so much by Quixote or Quijana as by those who are moved and transformed by his insanity. The play ends with the other prisoners singing "The Impossible Dream" to Cervantes as he is being led away for judgment before the Inquisition. It's powerful stuff, and that is why the play has captured the hearts of so many people all over the world."

"But Craig was no Cervantes."

"No. Craig, I'm afraid, was too lightweight for that. Craig, I would say, was the demented knight."

"Acting out what?"

"His dementia."

"And that took the form of . . . ?"

"One of the boys who was in the play is very shy. He's a bit overweight and has a so-so talent but he'll make it in community theater if he sticks it out. Well, this boy fell crazy in love with one of the girls in the chorus. Talked about her all the time, I gather, among the other guys, but he was too shy to even ask the girl for a date. So Craig-Quixote intervened. He didn't play John Alden, he played God.

"Told the boy that he'd overheard the girl talking about him, that she was crazy about him and that she couldn't understand why the boy wasn't showing any interest in her. Well, I'm sure he was kindly motivated and thought it would give the boy the courage to make a move. Instead, the boy asked Craig to make the move for him. Craig did, apparently, but the girl said the same thing that Priscilla said, speak for yourself.

"So Craig made a date with her, then went back and told the boy that it was all set up. So the boy goes and blows a hundred and fifty dollars for a limousine and shows up at the girl's door at the appointed hour bearing flowers and candy. Predictably, she is very disappointed by this turn of events and slams the door in the boy's face. We heard about this from the girl herself. Never saw the boy again. He was too humiliated to come back, even quit the show by telephone."

I said, "A good deed gone astray."

"Worse than that," Judith assured me. "I called Craig on that. He just smiled at me and said, 'He had it all for awhile, didn't he?' That's what I mean about confusing dreams with reality. That boy didn't have anything except a false hope that turned to ashes very quickly. But Craig saw it as something else."

"He saw it as . . . ?"

"As something experienced in the mind, something that was very real in the mind for awhile. Something very joyous, a dream come true."

"But only in the mind."

"Right."

"Like Quixote's mind when he attacks a windmill and believes that he has vanquished a dragon."

"Exactly."

"But that works in the play. It worked in the novel."

"It works," she told me, "because Quixote never knows that he's a dream and because Alonso never awakens from it. But what will become of Cervantes when he finally faces the Inquisition? You see, the play ends without answering that question."

"What happens to the dream," I asked soberly, "when the dreamer disappears?"

"Exactly," she said. "Does it have a life of its own? No. The dream vanishes with the dreamer."

"And those left behind," I mused aloud, "have to sort it all out."

"If that is what you are trying to do," she said quietly, "then good luck."

"Maybe Craig himself was a dream."

"Then who was the dreamer?"

"Maybe," I said, "a kid from Minnesota. Ever hear the name Alfred Johansen?"

"Sure," she said immediately. "He's in the play but he uses the stage name Johnny Lunceford. He and Craig are best friends. He's the Padre in the play but he also understudies Craig in the title role."

I didn't know if I was glad or sad over that news. I just knew that the stage of possibilities was becoming very, very crowded.

CHAPTER 13

WE TALKED A bit more and Judith named the three actors who'd followed Craig Maan from the theater on the night he was killed. The four were close friends and apparently the only thing Craig had said at the theater before he walked out was, "That's it, I'm sorry but I'm out of it and I'm out of here."

The three had followed him outside to find out what was wrong and none of them had returned.

Judith knew nothing about a secret marriage between Craig and Elaine and doubted that the story was true. As far as she knew, Craig had not dated any of the girls in the show and did not seem to be particularly interested in any.

I saw sheriff's cars parked outside the theater as I was walking Judith back from the coffee shop so I did my thanks and goodbye outside and went on to my car. That didn't change anything because Art Lahey was parked alongside and waiting for me.

"Get in," he said, without a greeting of any kind.

So I got into his car and we drove away without another word between us.

He headed east along Foothill Boulevard then turned north. It seemed that we were traveling toward the murder scene. "What's up?" I finally asked him.

"Just shut up," he replied.

So I just shut up and let it develop his way. After a moment he glanced at me and asked, "Did you get anything from Miss White?"

"It seems," I said, "that the victim qûit the show and walked out with two minutes notice. Three of his friends followed to see what was wrong. None of them returned. She had to patch the show up with those that were left."

Lahey grunted then asked me, "Which victim?"

"How many victims do we have?" I countered.

"We'll see," he said.

"I was talking about Craig Maan. The other three are Sanchez, Peterson and Stein."

"What about Miss Suzanne?"

I replied, "I gave you that last night."

"Give it again."

I said, "She did the show last night. I was there. She was on stage practically the whole time. She slipped me a note to meet her at the stage door after the show. I did, and we went looking for Maan. She—"

"That was about what time?"

"Shortly after eleven o'clock."

"And Maan was last seen at . . . ?"

"It's an eight-thirty curtain."

"So about three hours later you found him dead."

"About that, yeah."

"You called it in immediately."

"Yeah. Well, within a couple of minutes. The girl was

overcome so I took her back to the car. Then I went straight back inside and called it in."

"The log shows the call received at eleven thirty-three."

"Sounds like it," I said.

"So you had just met her for the first time about thirty minutes earlier."

"That's right."

"Even so, you made a pitch on her behalf and took responsibility for her, took her away."

I said, "It seemed the thing to do, Art. She was a client, sort of."

"So you said. You took her to your own doctor. Why not to the emergency room?"

"You know how that goes. We'd have been there all night. My doctor was closeby, and it took five minutes."

"What medication did the doctor give her?"

"Think she said it was seconal. I still have a couple of the pills at home, probably, in the clothes I was wearing last night. What's this all about, Art?"

"Just shut up."

I said, "Fuck you, don't ask me a thousand questions you've already asked and then tell me to shut up. Where are we headed?"

"We'll see."

But I already knew, I thought, where we were headed. We were near Rancho Cucamonga by then and approaching the apartment complex where I'd found the body of Craig Maan.

But I was in for a bit of a surprise. We went on past the scene of that crime and whipped around a corner to another section of the complex.

It looked very much the same as the other. Yellow tape was strung about the outside of the building and there were cops all over the place.

I asked Lahey, "What the hell is this?"

"Guess," he said.

"That's all I've done for three days," I told him.

"Then you shouldn't mind a few minutes more," he growled.

But I did. I minded it all to hell.

Four more murder victims were at that scene. And I recognized them all.

All were nude, three guys and a gal, and if you could believe the evidence, they'd all died in the midst of a sexual orgy. Blood was everywhere throughout that small apartment, spattered onto the walls and even the ceilings though all four bodies lay in a heap on a large waterbed. Drug paraphernalia were scattered about, as were small plastic packets of a white powder that looked like cocaine. A video camera was positioned on a tripod near the bed with the power still on and the monitor displaying the hellish scene, although the VCR to which the camera was attached was not now functioning.

All four victims had been repeatedly slashed and stabbed.

I identified them as Elaine Suzanne, Peter Stein who played Pedro, Jesus Sanchez who played Sancho—Quixote's faithful manservant—and James Peterson, one of the Muleteers.

I asked Lahey, "Is there a tape in that VCR?"

"Seems to be," he replied. "We'll let the forensics people check it out. Don't you touch a damned thing in here."

I was not about to touch a damned thing in there, didn't want my prints left on any of it.

"How long dead?" I asked him.

"Don't know yet. The call came down just before I picked you up. Hasn't been time for the coroner to respond. What would you say?"

I'm no forensics expert but I'd seen enough stiffs in my time to guess. "Quite awhile. Can we get out of here?"

"Lost your stomach for it, Joe?" Lahey asked quietly.

"Never developed one," I told him.

We went outside and stood in the grass to await the forensics team. Lahey went over to talk with one of the uniformed deputies, jotted some details in his notebook, then came back to tell me, "Next door neighbor reported it. Leaving for work, saw the door ajar, remembered hearing strange sounds during the night, investigated. I'm going to go talk to her. Want to come along?"

I growled, "Thanks, yeah," and went along.

Glad I did.

It seemed to be a favored area for the impossible dream people.

I recognized this girl too. And I'd finally found my whisperer.

CHAPTER 14

I WOULD NOT have recognized this kid as Antonia, the pretty niece of Alonso, and I had to wonder if I'd actually seen her in the role, but I did get an instant memory make from the mug shot in the cast file and knew that she was Susan Baker before Lahey spoke the name.

"Miss Baker?" He showed her his badge. "I am Sergeant Lahey of the San Bernadino Sheriff's Department. Can we come in and talk to you?"

She was a sizzler. Looked about eighteen but I knew better than that. Great body, long and lithe but nicely plumped out in all the right places, enticingly provocative now in a skintight leotard—dark flashing eyes, olive-cream complexion, jet black hair all wild and touseled and falling below the shoulders. But that doesn't tell it all. Something else was woven into all that, some kind of wild energy or essence. She smouldered, that was it, as though something vital and commanding was boiling up inside and slowly escaping through her pores—a controlled explosion.

Lahey was visibly affected by it and I guess I was too.

She swung the door wide and leaned into it, almost like a studied pose yet natural and graceful, and motioned us inside with her leg. "Sure, come on in," she said in a hoarse whisper. She raised a manicured hand to her throat. "Sorry, it's laryngitis, the singer's curse. I can stand it if you can."

Then she saw me and did a double take over the shoulder as she retreated into the apartment, glowered at me while Lahey and I took seats, then she did one of those quick switches, showed me a weak little smile and said, "Hi, Joe."

I smiled back. "Hi, kid."

Lahey sent a questioning look between us and asked, "Do you two know each other?"

I told him, "Miss Baker plays Antonia in *Man of La Mancha*."

He turned to her with a hard look and said, "So you recognized the victims next door."

"No," she replied, returning his riveting gaze full on. "I just stood in the doorway and peeked inside. All the lights were on and the door was standing open. I didn't see anyone to recognize, just blood splattered all around." Her gaze fled to me. "So I came right back over here and called 911."

She had one of those faces that couldn't seem to hold a focus for more than a second or two. Various expressions were on a constant march across it, as though reflecting tumbling thoughts behind it. There were a lot of jerky little body movements too—head up, head down, head to one side and then another, shoulders up, shoulders down, legs crossed and a foot swinging, ankles crossed, legs scissored to her torso and both feet up, then one and then the other—all this in a restless and relentless attempt to match the outer with the inner and never quite succeeding.

"But you did know the tenants next door," Lahey persisted.

"Sure. I found the apartment for them. Never dreamed they'd be lousy neighbors." She smiled to herself and drew a foot up under her on the couch, then decided she'd rather sit on the other one, settled for both as she continued. "Peter, James and Jesus." She did not give it the Spanish pronunciation, *Hay-soose*. "I call them the trinity." She giggled "Is that awful? Well, what the hell, I'm an infidel. So burn me." One arm curled over the head, the other hand gripping a foot. "What was going on over there last night?—a cock fight?" She squealed and hastened to explain, "No, I mean like, you know, roosters—gamecocks."

Lahey glanced at me, frowned, told her, "This is a murder investigation, Miss Baker. You weren't aware that—?"

She'd leapt from the couch and turned to me to ask, "Which one was murdered, Joe?"

I looked at Lahey. His eyes told me to go ahead, so I told her, "All were murdered, kid."

"Craig too?"

I nodded. "Him first."

She danced over to a hall closet and pulled out a jacket, put it on and said, "Well, I'm late for work."

Lahey went over to block the door, asked her, "You have to be at the theater this early?"

She replied, "No, I have to be at my real job this early. I'm a dance-aerobics instructor. I'm really quite late. I have to leave now."

"We'll make this as brief as possible," he assured her.

"No, you don't understand. I have to go right now."

The kid appeared to be very disoriented. She tried to get past Lahey and couldn't, glanced at me and went the other way, began moving aimlessly about the room in jerky movements and talking incoherently.

Lahey opened the door and put his head outside, called for a paramedic. I was trying to get an arm around the kid and she kept throwing it off, acting crazy but not violently so.

A paramedic came in and put her down, examined her, then hit her immediately with a needle.

Reality can be a bit too hard to take, I guess, when it begins to look too much like the nightmare. Susan Baker's dream had turned into that, for sure.

"We'll have to transport her," the paramedic informed us.

"Where to?" Lahey asked him.

"The nearest psycho ward. Guess that would be Valley Central."

"Treat her with respect," I growled.

"I treat all psychos with respect," the guy growled back.

But I didn't think that Susan Baker was a psycho. I decided that she was simply terrified.

It appeared that I was out of Lahey's dog house—for the moment anyway. He told me that he was running Craig Maan's fingerprints and hoped to have a solid ID before the day was over, also that he had already flashed them to all the local police agencies just in case there was anything to the story that Maan had worked as an undercover cop.

I wished him well in all that but told him also that I thought the FBI could provide that ID any time they wanted to. He didn't argue with that; it almost seemed as though he knew something that he wasn't ready to share with me, so I just let it go.

I told him, too, about the curious story of Alfred Johansen alias Johnny Lunceford and the Minnesota connection. Told him I thought the feds were behind it, that it seemed very strange to me that someone would try to confuse Johansen/Lunceford with Maan/Whoever unless the idea was disinformation and the goal was to sidetrack me completely.

He said, "Sidetrack you from what?"

I said, "'There's the brass ring, pal. What is it and who's got it? I don't know, but I feel that I have to run it down."

Then I told him about the "cruelest lie" that had turned the *La Mancha* cast upside down, and I pointedly mentioned Larry Dobbs and Jack Harney, adding that I was considering the possibility that Maan had used the story to explain the presence of Dobbs and Harney, without regard to the effect of that cruel deception upon his friends.

Lahey advised me, with a warning in his voice, "Don't put too much stock in that angle, Joe."

I asked him, "So what do you know that I should know about that?"

He replied, "I'm not so sure that anyone was even watching Maan."

"Bullshit," I said. "That's why Dobbs and Harney have been laying all over me. They—" I saw something in Lahey's eyes that made me think again. "—okay, if they weren't watching Maan, who were they watching?"

He signalled for a uniformed deputy, told him, "Take Mr. Copp back to his car."

I couldn't give it up that easy. "What about Elaine Suzanne? How do you think she got here? That hit on my place had Dobbs and Harney written all over it. One of them suckered me away with gunfire while the other snatched the girl. Why? Why did they want the girl?"

"The officer will take you to your car, Joe."

"Put a guard on the whisperer! I mean it!"

"Joe . . ."

"Do me one thing! Run a make on Dobbs and Harney. Give me a handle on those guys. Get me an address, a phone number, anything!"

"Maybe later," he said with a sigh. "Right now I have to put these other pieces together. Five people died here last night, at different times and different apartments but in the same complex and they're all linked to one another by friendship and by work. At the moment I don't know who did it or why but I intend to find out. So just stay out of my way, Joe. When I know something for sure, I'll let you know."

"Talk to Dobbs and Harney," I insisted.

He merely nodded his head at that and walked away. I slid into the police cruiser, grinned at the deputy, and said, "Nice guy."

"Sergeant Lahey?" The deputy smiled and started the engine. "We call him Bulldog. Once he gets his teeth into it, he never lets go. And he is *not* a nice guy."

I knew that.

Sure, I knew that. And I was damned glad he wasn't.

CHAPTER 15

NO MATTER HOW many times you've walked the valleys of the shadow, no matter how professional you may be or try to be, you never get blasé about violent death, it is never a minor concern—and I'd just been in a hell house. I give you that so you'll know my state of mind at the time and so you'll understand when I tell you that I probably was not running on all my cylinders as I left that place.

It isn't merely the sight and smell of death that rattles the brain in a scene like that one. Something more vivid than sight and more evocative than smell broods over the charnel house, something oppressive and threatening—like dread, only this is not a quality of mind but a physical reality that depressees the senses and heightens that other sense, the sixth sense as some would call it—a sort of *knowingness* of horror.

I've been told that psychics and other sensitives can sometimes develop intelligence from that atmosphere, decipher it and even reconstruct to fine detail the events that transpired there. If that is true, then it would suggest that something like memory overhangs scenes of incredible violence, that it somehow becomes impressed or recorded upon the physical structure that surrounds the events.

I would not find that difficult to swallow because I know that violent death leaves its imprints behind, one way or another, and that it affects any normal person who is exposed to it.

And I was thinking about my whisperer, Susan Baker, and trying to understand her behavior. Had she been lying when she said that she had not been inside the apartment of death?—that she had not known what had happened there? If she'd been telling the truth about that, would she have reacted the way she did when I told her what had happened there?

There are different strokes for different folks, I understand that, and I had no past familiarity with Susan to use as a guide—but I'd seen hundreds of other folks over the years in their reactions to similar situations, and I had to grade Susan's reaction as *bizarre* . . . if she'd told the truth.

Of course if she'd been in there . . . during or after the fact—then the nervous breakdown or whatever it was could be easily explained as a delayed reaction to overpowering horror . . . or guilt. Whichever and whatever, I felt that I had to follow up on Susan Baker and learn the truth about her. That would not be easy to do. I'd seen the same questions in Lahey's eyes and knew that he would be keeping her under close wraps, at least for awhile.

Meanwhile I still had her thousand bucks so I felt sort of obligated to see that she was treated fairly and properly.

That is the state I was in when the deputy dropped me at my car. We had met two other sheriff's cars on their way out of the theater area; I stood there outside my car gazing indecisively at the open stage door, then decided what the hell and went inside for another go at Judith White.

It was now a bit past nine o'clock and several people were fooling around backstage, messing with the scenery and whatever. Judith was in her office, reared back in the swivel chair with feet crossed atop the desk, hands folded behind her head and staring fixedly at the ceiling.

I stood just inside the door and said to her, "I've heard that all the world's a stage. Does that include ceilings?"

She replied in a dreamy voice without breaking the pose. "Sure does. There's a big playwright in the sky, I think, and every play is a play within a play. So what the heck is it all about?"

I went on in and sat down on the casting couch, glanced at the ceiling, told her, "Solve just one piece of it, kid. Then use that as a template."

"You've been solving pieces of it all your life," she said in the same dreamy voice. "What did it ever get you?"

"Nice place in the hills," I replied. "My car is paid for. Old, but paid for. I eat okay, usually. Even take in a play now and then."

"Did it ever get you a wife?"

"A few, yeah, briefly."

"Why didn't you use your template on them?"

"Too wriggly," I said. "They wouldn't hold still for it."

She cocked her head to look at me. "You're not so bad, I guess."

"Gee, thanks. Neither are you."

"I mean you sort of grow on. I'll bet inside that tough armor beats a very gentle heart. I'll bet you're not half as tough as you look."

I shrugged and made a tough face. "Guess you can't fool all the people all the time."

She laughed softly and brought her feet down, sat up

straight and smoothed her hair, said, "My day is shot to hell. The worse part, I don't seem to care. I was thinking about Craig."

"Yeah?"

"Yes. Yesterday was so full of promise. And also anxiety. And also . . . just so *full* of everything. For Craig, I mean. Okay, he was full of bullshit. But even *that* is something. Where is all that now?"

I replied, "Wherever Craig is now, I guess. I think you do take it with you."

"Where?"

"To the next theater, maybe."

"What do you want, Joe?"

"Everything I can get, I guess."

"No, I meant . . . what are you doing here?"

"Came to tell you something."

"Okay. Please tell it and get out. I am feeling very small right now, completely ineffectual, and I might just start crying at any minute."

I got up and went to the door. "Then I'd better not tell you."

"Is it about Craig?"

"No. It's about—well, first I'd like to ask a question."

She made a wry face, said, "I take it back, you're not okay. You are designing and manipulative. But go ahead. Ask your damn question."

"How long has Susan had laryngitis?"

"What?"

"Antonia, Susan Baker. How long has she been out of the play?"

She blinked at me. "All week. Why?"

"How well do you know her?"

"Well enough to avoid her outside this theater. Susan is a total flake."

"In what way?"

"In every way. Thinks she's the reincarnation of Sarah Bernhardt. I mean literally. Always talking about past lives, all that stuff. She has screwed every boy in the cast, trying to find her soul mate."

I grinned. "Sounds like a good place to start."

Judith tossed her head and said, "I believe she's tried a couple of the girls too. Says we come back into different sexes, have to experience it all before we can escape karma. That's a pretty good cop-out for nymphomania."

"Would you say that she is not of sound mind?"

"Nothing wrong with her mind," Judith sniffed. "It's a problem in character, I fear."

"She's gotten it on with all the guys?"

"There are probably a few exceptions. Susan doesn't have the right plumbing for several of these boys."

"Would those several be Peter, James and Jesus?"

She gave me a sharp look. "What are you getting at?"

"They lived next door to her, didn't they?"

She stared a hole through me before replying, "Lived? Past tense?"

I broke contact with those brooding eyes and said, "Yeah, 'fraid so."

"Well that's a rotten trick!" she cried.

"What's a rotten trick?"

"You're trying to tell me that Susan is dead? After you just made me say all those terrible things? Joe, that is rotten."

I went back and sat down on the couch. "Susan isn't dead, Judith."

"Well thank God for something!" she said, fuming in relief. "Guess I'm ready to believe anything." She impaled me again with those hot eyes. "So just what are you getting at?"

"Susan was hospitalized this morning. Nervous breakdown or something."

"Over Craig?"

I shrugged. "Well . . ."

"Well what?"

"Craig and the others."

"What others?"

I got up off the couch again and she met me in the middle of the room. "The deputies didn't tell you?"

"No, dammit, what others?"

I took both her arms and said, "Calm down. This is going to be rough. Susan stumbled onto it this morning as she was leaving for her day job. All three of the guys next door were killed sometime during the night. I think it was some time after Craig died, and only about a block away."

Shock, you know, is something like anesthesia. It's like a circuit breaker designed to disconnect the emotional circuits when they become overloaded.

I saw the precise moment when Judith White's circuit breaker tripped, saw the eyes bland out and felt the body go limp.

I was hanging onto her to keep her upright and I didn't know if she heard the rest of it or if it registered in the mind.

"Either they were having a sex party or someone wanted it to look that way. There was a girl with them. It was Elaine Suzanne. She's dead too."

"Susan killed them," Judith said in a barely audible voice.

I said, "Well, no, I didn't say that."

She was going to pure liquid, laying against me in a vertical position. It was terrible, I know—considering the circumstances—but I was strongly aware of the warmth of that lovely body on mine.

"Get me out of here," she whispered.

"Where would you like to go?"

"Just get me out. Out of here. Take me home."

"Yours or mine?"

She got her feet under her again at that point, pushed gently away from me, raked me with eyes that were coming alive again. "Yours," she said.

So I took her to my castle in the hills, and we built a lovely stage far above it all, and co-wrote the sweetest play of all. Happens that way sometimes, without plan or direction, and nobody is to blame. Call it anesthesia.

CHAPTER 16

IT WAS WILD, it was crazy and it consumed the rest of the morning plus a tad of the early afternoon. When finally we were both too exhausted to answer another curtain call, I slithered away and staggered to the shower wondering what had God wrought. Judy—right, Judy—called after me from the bed in a breathless but still taunting voice, "That's what you get for taking a sex-starved girl to bed."

Yeah right, I was thinking, and I must have gotten it all.

She showered while I whipped up Spanish omelettes in the kitchen, came out wrapped in one of my terrycloth robes and perched prettily on a chair at the table just as I was turning the omelettes out of the pan, seemed bright and perky, playful even, no hint of post-passion embarrassment. She gazed at her plate and sniffed the air, patted my bottom as I moved away.

"Do you do everything well, Joe?" she asked in a small, barely audible voice, "or have I just caught you in your strongest suits?"

"Better taste it first," I suggested and pulled up a chair across from her.

Ever notice how some women get prettier after sex while

some seem less so? Has something to do with the set of the face, and maybe that's influenced by something different behind the face, I don't know, don't quote me on that. All I know for sure is that this one was definitely prettier and that is saying something because she was a beauty to start. I'm not talking about the look of ecstasy—that's a sure winner for every woman, I've never seen one that wasn't beautiful in ecstasy—I'm talking about later, after all the fires have been damped and she's coming back into the real world again.

She said, "I've embarrassed you."

I grinned and replied, "That's okay, embarrass me again. Just how well am I?"

"Well enough," she said with a purr in the voice. "This is the best omelette I've ever had."

"Oh, *that* suit."

She laughed softly and we finished the food in silence but with a lot of smiles and charged looks across the table. I got up to refill our cups with coffee and told her as I sat down again, "I'll bet you're a great actress."

She pushed her plate away and toyed with the coffee for a little while before replying, "That was no act, Joe."

"Course it wasn't, wasn't talking about that," I said. "I meant the stage."

"I don't want to talk about that."

I said, "Okay."

"Anyway, I'm more of a singer and dancer than an actress. More a dancer than a singer."

I grinned at that. "Oh, I know you're a great dancer."

She giggled and said, "Stop it."

I said, "No, let's not. Now that you've got some food in you, you want to try that one more time?"

She went serious, said, "Can I have a rain check?"

"You got it," I said. "Good any time."

Actually I hadn't meant to pump her for information, after all that, but it was her idea to talk about it, she brought it up, lips pursed and brow all furrowed in thought: "What is going on, Joe? Why all these killings?"

So, hell. I told her, "I don't know, kid. But I'd sure like to find out. I could be in big trouble if I don't."

"What do you mean? What kind of trouble?"

I did not tell Judith everything but I did tell her what I meant by that—the mysterious way I'd been hired to protect Craig, the instant reaction via gunfire outside the theater, the hostile visit by Dobbs and Harney and the kidnap-rape setup, the thing with Elaine and Lahey's reaction to that—the nude photo of me found at the murder scene—I gave her all that stuff and finished with, "So you can see, there's enough circumstantial incrimination to make me feel very uneasy about all this. I've been a cop long enough to know better than to just sit back and let the cops figure it out. I know exactly how Lahey is pursuing this investigation. He's taking it by the numbers, like all good cops do, but sometimes those numbers get scrambled and you never know what will emerge in the final picture. Figures don't lie, right. Liars figure, though, and that's the worry. The Polaroid snapshot of me that Lahey found under Craig's body was taken more than two weeks ago. Why would anyone sneak into a public gym and snatch a picture that way unless it would fit into some devious plot that was already being hatched at the time?"

Judith brooded on that one for a moment before replying, "Gay boys have pinups. I've seen a few on locker doors in my time. Not that I'm suggesting . . ." She made a tiny smile. "But I guess you could turn the boys on, Joe."

I ignored that. "Was Craig gay?"

She looked away, studied the wall for a moment, looked back at me to say, "I don't know. Some of his best friends are."

"The three . . . ?"

She nodded. "Bi, anyway. Look—I never ask anyone what they do in the bedroom with whom, that's private and I'm not even interested in knowing. But you've got to understand—maybe you already do—gay men as a rule seem to be much more sensitive, often highly creative and perhaps even more gifted on the average than straight men. They naturally gravitate toward the arts . . . and there are a lot of them in theater. I learned that a long time ago." She showed me a rueful smile. "Got a few lessons the hard way but I don't want to talk about that. The point is, there's nothing unusual in the fact that some of our cast are gay. As for Craig . . . I just couldn't say. He seemed to enjoy the adoring attention of women but I don't know that he ever took any to bed. As for the other . . . it's not uncommon for straight actors to have gay friends. We sort of . . . pride ourselves on being very liberal that way."

I asked her, "Do you get the same proportion of gay women—lesbians?"

She gave me a direct look as she replied, "No, I think—this is just my own observation, for what it's worth—I think it might work the opposite way for women. Haven't you noticed?—Lesbians seem more attracted to the more aggressive lifestyles that have traditionally been the sphere of the strong male. Like, you know, competitive sports, executive careers, the law." She raised an eyebrow at me. "Law enforcement?"

I shrugged and said, "Maybe."

"But it wouldn't be fair to say that all female jocks and cops and business executives are lesbians, would it."

I told her, "I've never suggested that all actors are gay."

She said, "Well in this town that wouldn't be far off."

"Really?"

She laughed softly. "No, I'm just spouting the conventional wisdom. I hear it all the time. But it simply isn't true. Don't make Craig gay simply because he was on the stage."

"How 'bout the understudy?—Lunceford or Johansen or whoever?"

She said very quickly, "Oh no, he's very happily married and is about to become a poppa."

"About how soon?"

She studied the wall again. "Oh . . . I think she's about six months along. They got married, uh, I understand, after the fact."

"He's a pretty solid guy?"

She nodded. "Seems to be. Works a regular day job forty hours a week yet never misses a performance. Johnny is more than an understudy, you know. He's also cast as the Padre, works every night."

I told Judith, then, about the Minnesota connection and asked her, "Did he ever talk to you about the family back home?"

She smiled. "Yes. We have something in common."

"What's that?"

"His father is a judge. So's mine."

I probably dropped a jaw on that one.

Judith showed me a funny look and asked, "What's wrong?"

"What kind of judge?" I muttered.

She shook her head. "I'm not sure. He refers to his dad as Judge Johansen, sort of jokes about it. I'd never joke about that. I'm proud of my dad."

"Is your dad a federal judge?"

"Sure is. U.S. District Court, California Central, sits in Los Angeles."

"Holy mackeral," I whispered.

"But uh, Joe, don't get any ideas. I couldn't possibly ask my dad to intervene in any . . ."

She'd misread my reaction. I was getting plenty of ideas, all right, but not the kind Judith thought. And I was mentally kicking my butt all around that kitchen. But after all, it's a common name and . . .

Judge White had been in the news quite a bit lately. He was hearing a red hot case—a racketeering case loaded with political fireworks and . . .

I told the judge's daughter, "I'm afraid there's already been an intervention, kid."

Yeah. And five of her associates were dead.

How many more would it take?

CHAPTER 17

THAT LITTLE BOLT of light cast the events of the past few days in a totally new perspective. Since the talk with my friend in the FBI, I'd been proceeding under a false presumption. I'd assumed that the guy had leveled with me—even while wondering about his willingness to do that. Friendships are nice and trust is beautiful but some things simply cannot be included in the package—and I'd been wondering all along, at the back of the mind, why a Special Agent of the FBI would say anything to anyone that might endanger the security of a federal witness. Why had he told me that?

It seemed obvious now that he'd merely dragged a red herring across the scene, and he'd done it skillfully. I'd been staggering around in the dark ever since.

I had leaped to the conclusion that Dobbs and Harney were Deputy United States Marshals assigned to protect a federal witness and that the witness was Craig Maan. Nobody had told me that but it was a natural conclusion in context with the other developments.

Then a simple, innocent statement by one whom I'd thought to be only peripherally involved changed the entire picture. I was stunned by that, and I instantly saw Dobbs and Harney in a totally new light.

Those guys had been there to protect Judith White.

So where were they now?

I had not seen them since early the previous evening—before my meeting with Elaine Suzanne, before discovery of the murder of Craig Maan, before any of that. They'd chased me outside during the overture and hastily cancelled a confrontation with me outside the theater upon learning that Craig Maan was not appearing that night. I'd naturally assumed that they were concerned about Maan's safety. If not that, then what? Where had they gone? And where were they now?

Obviously Judith had known nothing about any of it. Even after I'd outlined the case for her . . .

Unless . . .

I asked her, "Have you been straight with me?"

She frowned as she replied, "What do you mean? Straight about what?"

"About everything, all of it. You've actually believed all this time that Larry Dobbs and Jack Harney were here to take *La Mancha* on the road? You never had a clue that they were anything else?"

She said, "Well . . . sometimes it's easier to take Craig at face value and let it go. But I've wondered—sure, I've wondered about it. We're closing *La Mancha* next week in any event, so . . ."

"When was the last time you talked to your dad?"

"My dad? I talk to him often. Why?"

I said, "Dammit, let me ask the questions for now. When did you last talk to him?"

She screwed her face in search for the answer, told me,

"I guess it was Monday. We're dark Mondays—I mean, no show. We had dinner. I was trying to remember if we'd talked on the phone since then, but I guess not. It was Monday."

"And he told you . . . ?"

She smiled. "The same thing he always tells me. Find a nice man. Make babies. Live like a human being. Mom died when I was sixteen. I keep turning the advice back on him. He's still a young man, he's handsome, successful. I tell him to find a nice woman. What is this, Joe? What does my father have to do with any of this?"

I didn't want to scare her. At the same time, I felt that she had a right to know if her life may be in danger. So I told her, "Your dad is hearing a very sensitive case. Vincent DiCenza is up on racketeering and bribery charges. He—"

"I know. I've seen it on the news."

"Your dad hasn't discussed the case with you?"

She made a face. "Never once in my whole life, not any case, even the very subject is taboo."

I said, "DiCenza has organized crime ties. He's considered to be one of the West Coast bosses."

"Yes, I've heard that."

"All the pundits are saying that he is going to buy some hard time this time. Your dad has been called a hanging judge."

She nodded. "Dad has always been tough on professional criminals."

"Have you been keeping up with the case?"

Judith replied, "From a distance, yes. I'm always interested in my dad's court cases. But that trial is over, it's been over for weeks. It's in the sentencing phase now."

I told her, searching my own memory of recent newspaper stories, "He's hearing defense motions this week. There are rumors of a deal. A light sentence in exchange for DiCenza's cooperation in other cases involving some highly placed politicians."

She was giving me a perplexed look. "So?"

"So Dobbs and Harney work out of the Central District Court of California. They could be working for your dad."

She turned her face into half-profile and sent me a crackling gaze from that angle. "What could Craig have to do with the DiCenza case?"

I looked away from those eyes to say, "Probably nothing whatever."

"So why would they be . . . ?" Her voice trailed off, she left her chair and walked once around the table, murmured, "Just a minute," and went into the bedroom.

She came back a minute later fully dressed and said to me, "You'd better take me back to the theater, Joe. It's getting late, and we do have a show to stage tonight."

I told her, "Don't be crazy."

She told me, "Don't you be crazy."

"Show must go on?"

She nodded. "Short of an earthquake, sure."

I sighed and went to get into my clothes. She was a tough lady. But Vin DiCenza was a very tough hood. And the tough get tougher when the situation is desperate.

Sure. There had already been an earthquake—or its equivalent—for five people very close to the judge's daughter.

I was beginning to think of each of those as a messenger, carrying their own message.

And I had already begun to experience a lot of sympathy for Larry Dobbs and Jack Harney.

I stalled Judith long enough to quietly call Art Lahey and ask him to meet me at the theater. He agreed, and he was waiting in his car when we arrived. I drove slowly past him and gave him a little sign to let him know that I'd spotted him then I pulled into a red zone at the curb near the stage door and walked Judith inside.

"You can't stay, Joe," she protested. "I have a hundred things to do."

"I know," I said. "Just want to check it out before I leave you."

The lady was no dummy; she knew what I meant and she didn't give me an argument. It was only mid-afternoon, five hours before showtime—but the room would begin to fill up at about six. They drew from the entire L.A. basin for these shows and probably half of every audience was composed of senior citizens groups who came by bus and van—and the old move deliberately on very loose schedules, so most of those were on hand when the doors opened at six o'clock.

We'd talked in the car coming down and Judith had told me that she wanted to contact each surviving member of the cast and get them in at least an hour early. The changes she'd made the night before would hold up okay but since then she'd also lost her female lead and they'd already been limping without Susan Baker in the lineup.

I suggested that perhaps it would be more fitting and certainly more seemly to simply close the show and stay dark for the remainder of the run, considering the tragedies. Judith would not even consider the idea. She told me, "These kids are going to be very distraught when they hear what has happened."

I said, "Yeah, that's what I meant."

"Going dark would compound the loss," she argued. "The best thing we can do is make an announcement to the audience, ask for a moment of silence to honor our dead, then go out there and knock 'em dead in their seats. That is what show biz is all about."

"Maybe so," I said, "but—"

"No buts," she declared firmly. "That's exactly what we're going to do."

So what the hell. I walked around the darkened theater, looked in the kitchen which was already bustling with activity, and went out for my meeting with Lahey.

He was standing outside and leaning against his car with arms folded at the chest, and he didn't look very happy. I told him right off the top, "You're in the big time now, pal, so you'd better trot your best people out here and get a handle on this situation. Forget everything I've told you about this case. I've been describing the sideshow. The main act just walked into that building with me and I believe that the show has only just begun. Judith White is Judge White's daughter. He's the one on the DiCenza case. I think what we've been seeing is a squeeze play on the judge. I believe that every one of our deaths last night was intended as a reminder to the judge of how vulnerable his daughter is. I think Dobbs and Harney are probably dead somewhere. I think some subtle threat must have been handed to the judge as soon as the guilty verdict came down, and I think that's why the marshals were out here. Well, they're not here anymore. But Judith White is, and

I can't convince her that she needs to find sanctuary somewhere. She's going on with the show tonight. I'd like to see a platoon of deputies surrounding this place and I'd like to see a couple of your best policewomen living inside Judith's shoes until we break this thing."

Lahey had been regarding me with melancholy eyes throughout that monologue. When I ran out of words he asked me, "Are you finished?"

I said, "For now."

He said, "No—you're finished, period. Dobbs and Harney are not dead, they're in jail. I put them there and the charge is murder. I'm taking you in too, Joe."

I said, "Get serious."

"You get serious." He pulled his gun and wagged it in the direction of the car. "Turn and spread, hands on the roof, you know the routine. You have the right to remain silent, you have the right . . ."

This guy was reading me my rights and he obviously had bought not a word of what I'd been telling him about Judith White.

I really didn't have an option.

I turned toward the roof of his car as though I was submitting but then I kept on spinning and kneed him in the groin, snatched the gun from his hand and banged it against the side of the head hard enough to put his lights out for a moment.

At least, I thought as I went to my car and put that scene behind me—at least there would be cops watching the area for awhile anyway.

Other than that, I didn't have a gasp of an idea of what I could do for Judith now. I just knew that I had to do something. And damned quick.

CHAPTER 18

DON'T GET THE idea that I was in a panic, or that I felt that Judith was in immediate danger of losing her life—but these guys in the big time play for keeps and seldom leave anything to chance. If I'd doped the case right and if DiCenza's people were trying to intimidate the judge by not-so-subtle threats against his daughter, then Judith very probably was not in immediate danger. To rub out five innocent bystanders is to send a very strong message, but the effect of that message depended on the judge's daughter being simply vulnerable, not dead.

And like I said, these people don't leave much to chance. My immediate worry was that they would quietly snatch the daughter and keep her on ice to insure that continuing state of vulnerability until they got what they wanted from her father.

Mind you, I was not one hundred percent convinced that I had all the answers to the thing but putting all the bits and pieces together from the DiCenza angle made the events of the past few days much more coherent when trying to draw a total picture. I still did not know what to make of the angle on Craig Maan and the reason for involving me in the thing—but sometimes it's too much to expect total coherency—sometimes dumb events intrude coincidentally upon sober events and serve only to cloud the picture, so I wasn't holding out for a neat package.

I had plenty enough to worry about with what I had, and what I had was a rather clear picture involving a federal judge and one of the biggest racketeers west of the Mississippi.

You have to understand the mentality at play here. In all their dealings, these people primarily rely on non-verbal communications. They don't say to you, "Cooperate or I'll kill you." Instead they kill someone close to you and that is supposed to be a metaphor for your own fate if you choose to oppose them. Or if you value that other life more highly than your own, they kill someone close to the other person and the message is the same.

These people would not directly threaten a federal judge, and they would not kidnap his daughter and send a ransom note. But someone somewhere at some opportune moment would find a way to indirectly suggest that the judge's daughter could be highly vulnerable to an attack by his enemies, and then they would show him by example how easy it would be.

They would wait then, to see if he comes around. How long the wait would depend on the urgency of their situation. But they'd wait long enough at least to check the effect of the message. If it didn't seem to be working—if this is a stubborn judge and he is moving to make his daughter less vulnerable—then the kidnap would be the logical next move.

That is what I was worried about. And I was worried, too, about the hanging judge. Maybe he would not submit to that kind of blackmail, not even with his daughter's life at stake—and maybe tempers would flare if all else failed and someone would decide to send that smart judge his daughter's head in a sack merely to teach him a lesson.

So, yes, in that assessment Judith was in very grave danger and the next shoe could drop at any time. Although I was not panicked, I also felt that it was no time to hem and haw over fine points of law with the official cop in the case while he runs along blind alleys in pursuit of a metaphor. That is why I smacked Art Lahey instead of letting him cuff me and haul me off to jail for no damned good reason at all. If I was right, I could square things later. If I was wrong, of course, then I'd probably worked my final case as a private cop in the state of California—or probably anywhere else.

But if I was right . . . then maybe I was Judith White's only hope for a happy outcome from this thing. It's not that I came to this big decision to risk life and career for a woman I barely knew. I knew her well enough, in the first place—how much better to know any woman than to spend three hours locked in her passionate embrace?—and if my primary interests were longevity and wealth I would not have picked this kind of work to begin with.

Hell, I'm a cop. Makes no difference whether the taxpayers or private clients are sponsoring me, I'm a cop. That's what I am and it's what I do.

And that is what I was doing when I smacked Lahey.

I traveled west through the foothills and ten minutes deep into L.A. county before I started looking for a public phone, and I called Judith first.

I told her briefly what had happened, and I told her

briefly about my worse fears, and then I urged her to get in touch with her father as quickly as possible.

"What am I supposed to tell him?"

"Tell him, dammit, that his lifeguards are behind bars in San Bernardino and that he should send replacements damned quick!"

"Oh God, Joe, I don't want to do that," she wailed. "He has enough on his mind already."

I couldn't believe it, and I told her that. I also told her, "The worse damned thing you can do is let yourself get snatched! Then they've got your dad by the ying-yang for sure! So if your concern is only for him . . ."

She said, "Maybe you're right."

"Damned right I'm right. Call him! Then you sit tight! Don't go anywhere without an escort. Stay right there! Understand?"

I guess she didn't. "Joe, this is silly. I can't spend the rest of my life with bodyguards."

"Maybe you won't spend the rest of your life with anyone then, and maybe you don't have a hell of a lot left to spend. Look!—Judith!—Judy, dammit!—this isn't a three-act play and you're not on a stage. It's real life and these people have shown us how little they value other people's real lives. They're playing to win and they will win if you try to just shrug it off."

She said, "Well . . ." in a very undecided tone of voice.

"I'm not asking you to go into hiding. I'm just telling you to be sensible. Use sensible caution. Don't expose yourself unnecessarily. Does that make sense?"

"I guess it does," she said. "I promise I'll call Daddy."

"And don't leave the theater without an escort."

"Joe . . ." Very undecided again.

I said, "Okay. Okay. I'll pick you up tonight."

"How will you do that? That sheriff will be looking for you, won't he?"

"Probably all the sheriffs are looking for me by now," I told her. "But I'll work it out. Wait for me."

"Okay."

"Promise."

"I promise. Where will you be in the meantime?"

I said, "Hell, I don't know."

"Why don't you go up to my place. Nobody would look for you there, would they?"

I thought about that for a second, then replied, "Maybe that's an idea. Where do you live and how do I get in?"

"Up near San Antonio Heights." She gave me the address and I jotted it on my palm. "Just ring the doorbell and tell Gertie who you are. I'll call ahead so she'll be expecting you."

"Who's Gertie?"

"The housekeeper. Don't worry, she's—"

"You've got a housekeeper?"

She laughed softly as she replied, "Well not out of my salary. Family money pays for the expenses on the house."

"You're living with your dad?"

"No, it's the old family home, Joe. Dad has a condo down in L.A." Her voice took on a kidding tone as she added, "Our lives are entirely separate and entirely our own . . . so maybe I'll pick up that rain check tonight."

I said, "Best offer I've had since uh . . . how long ago was it?—about noontime?"

She wasn't kidding anymore as she told me, "That was

really wild, Joe. Keeps bouncing back on me. Can't get you out of my head. What did you do to me?—spike my drink, or something? I've never . . ."

I told her, "Always takes two to tango, kid. But I'd be happy to compare notes with you later tonight."

"Deal," she said.

"So keep it intact."

"Keep what intact?"

"Keep that gorgeous ass intact with the rest of the equipment. Don't hang it out anywhere and invite someone to whack it off. 'Cause I don't want you without your ass, kid."

Judith hung up laughing, but I did not.

I was deadly serious, and even more so after I'd called Art Lahey.

I called for Lahey from the same public phone and I told the guy who picked it up, "If he's not on the line in thirty seconds I'm hanging up."

I got him in ten, and not in the best of humor.

Lahey growled, "I can't believe this, you crazy bastard."

"Start believing," I suggested, "and begin with the idea that I'm sincerely sorry that I had to conk you, then—"

"I can live with the conk. But I'll probably never make a baby again."

"You've made enough already," I told him. "Don't try to stall me, Art. I know how long it's safe to hang on here so forget it and let's talk to the point. You're on a false trail. I don't care what kind of evidence you've got, it's not what it looks like. You've got the DiCenza bunch in your territory now and they make what they want to make. Keep a guard on that girl and you'll be a hero. Don't, and you'll be the asshole they want you to be."

He said, "Speaking of assholes, we're pulling your license. And I just issued an APB. You're armed and dangerous, so don't expect any special handling when they throw you down."

I said, "I'm not armed, Art."

"You've got my pistol."

"Not me," I assured him. "I left it with you."

"Wasn't there when I came around."

"Then someone else is armed and probably much more dangerous," I told him. "Do you have some people down there at that God damned theater now?"

He said, "Enough that you'd better give it a wide berth, asshole."

"They'll come at you and right through you," I warned him. "I've dealt with people like these before, so don't put your cadets down there, these people don't play defensively. It's offense all the way and you'd better get ready for it."

I hung it up and got away from there.

So maybe I'd overplayed it just a bit. Then again, maybe not.

And maybe, I was thinking, I'd better take my own advice and make myself armed and dangerous.

CHAPTER 19

I WENT BACK east and circled south instead of north toward San Antonio Heights, wanted to run by Valley Central Hospital and try to look in on Susan Baker. That may sound crazy but I figured it was worth a soft probe anyway. I wasn't going to do anything crazy, just take a look and play the ear. Had no intention of spending the day at Judith's place in the hills either, though the idea was strong that I should go take a look there too and see what I could learn from the White family home. Didn't really know where else to start, and now with the added aggravation of trying to avoid cops it seemed a little silly to be running up and down the boulevards in Lahey country—but what the hell else could I do?

The hospital was on the way, sort of, and I wanted to see Susan Baker. Had absolutely no idea of what I would find there, if anything, but certainly Susan could be an important piece of the puzzle. If I could get to her, and if she could talk coherently to me . . . well I figured it was worth the risk. And I got lucky. A police car was standing empty outside the emergency entrance, but that's normal, you can expect to see that any time—and I could not detect any hint of other police presence in the area.

I waltzed in the back way and went up to the psychological/psychiatric section and walked smack into Susan—right past her door anyway, saw her sitting in bed watching television. She didn't see me and I didn't see anyone else in the room, nor was there any evidence that she was under any kind of security watch.

I went on to the nurse's station and told the girl at the desk, "I'm Doctor Joseph."

She looked up from a report and said, "Yes?"

"I'm consulting on Susan Baker."

She was quick on the uptake. "Oh yes. She was just brought down from the security ward. This way, please."

That told me something right there. It meant both that Susan was not considered a difficult patient and that the cops were no longer standing over her.

The nurse was leading me to Susan's room. I followed her back down the hallway, asked her from a pace behind, "What is the regimen?"

She replied over her shoulder as we continued along, "Bedrest and TLC. She's doing fine."

"No medication?"

"Nothing's on the chart. She will probably be released tomorrow."

The nurse left me at the door and I went into the room alone, which of course was what I wanted once I had established the condition of the patient.

Susan turned her head to look at me, blinked twice then said, "Oh, it's you." The voice sounded a bit weak but she wasn't whispering.

"You got your voice back," I observed.

"Yeah, how 'bout that."

I laid the thousand bucks on her bed tray and told her, "I didn't earn this."

She looked at the money for a moment before replying, "It's not all mine. How much did you earn?"

"Not a penny."

"I guess not." She turned her head toward the window. "I don't want the fucking money."

I said, "Maybe the other contributors wouldn't feel that way. Take it."

"They're all dead," she declared in a tiny voice.

"What kind of game was it, Susan?" I asked gently.

She turned to me with a snort. "Game?! Some game! They're all dead! All but me! Why not me?"

"Who killed them?"

Her eyes fled again to the window. "Craig said it would be easy, like learning a script and staging it. Well it was never easy. It was horrible. Nobody would cooperate. Everyone had to ad lib. Like you."

I said, "I guess no one ever showed me the script, kid. What was I supposed to do?"

"You were supposed to . . ." She caught herself and turned to me with venom in the eyes. "Get out of here!" she screamed.

I tried to calm her but it just got worse, at the top of her lungs.

The nurse was running back toward the room when I stepped outside.

"Guess she doesn't like me," I said as the nurse ran past me.

Damned if I knew why, though. Nice guy like me? My performance on Craig's stage must have been a terrible disappointment to everyone.

It was a graceful three-level house on a cul-de-sac with several others of equal value, probably built at a time when a hundred-thousand dollar house was a mansion and dirt was still cheap. With real estate now a cottage industry and everyone playing that market, you probably couldn't touch these places for a million—but it was the kind of home you would visualize for a successful lawyer. Don't know about federal judges—they're not in the same league because their annual salary wouldn't equal a lawyer's share of one good accident award—but I didn't know at the time how long Judge White had been on the bench or how long ago he'd bought the property.

The area was nicely secluded—deeper into the hills than where I lived and the terrain quite a bit more rugged—but it was a view house perched onto the side of the mountain, so there was not that feeling of isolation that comes with some of these remote neighborhoods.

Gertie was black, about sixty, obviously sharp of mind but also gentle and possessed of a dignified reserve, not terribly warm but not cold either—the perfect housekeeper. I gathered that she'd been with the family for a long time. I asked her about Judge White and she told me that he had moved into Los Angeles several years earlier, shortly after Judith returned home from her world travels.

"That's about the time he went on the bench," I guessed.

She said, "When he went to federal court, yes. He was a judge before that."

"Superior Court?"

She shrugged and made a dumb face. "It was just down here in Pomona, whatever that court is."

"Do you like him?"

"The judge? How could I not like the judge? He's a great man."

Gertie did not live in. She had a family in Ontario, worked a regular eight to five, forty hour week, and Judith had given her the rest of the day off after my arrival. I got the idea that she was anxious to leave. She showed me around the main level and pointed out the bar, the refrigerator loaded with goodies, fresh pot of coffee, the game room.

"Judith said you'd make yourself at home," she told me. "So if you don't need me for anything . . ."

I shooed her out, moved my car into the garage as soon as she drove away, and went back inside for an unguided tour.

I could not find Judith's imprint anywhere except in the master bedroom. It looked like her, in there. The rest of the house looked like a judge's house. I got the idea that Judith merely slept there.

The bookshelves in the library were lined with law books, the desk in the adjoining study was massive but served no currently useful purpose except as support for a telephone and a leather desk set, all the drawers totally bare.

I found myself wondering what the judge had in mind for this place. Retirement home? He had no clothing there or any other personal items. The upkeep, with housekeeper and all, must be tremendous. Granted, it would be a long commute into L.A. but . . .

Another smaller desk was in Judith's bedroom and I struck some paydirt there. Her telephone was one of the hi-tech automatic type with frequently-called phone numbers stored in memory for single-digit dialing. One of the stored numbers was for "Dad—Office"—another, "Dad—Condo."

I glanced at the clock and punched in Dad—Office. A female voice responded on the first ring: "Judge White's chambers."

I said, "This is Joe Copp. I'm a friend of Judith's. Tell him I'm on the line."

The judge came on line almost immediately and in a rich baritone great for the bench. "What can I do for you, Mr. Copp?"

I told him, "There's probably not much God himself can do for me right now, Your Honor, but I think there's a great deal you can do for your daughter. Did she call you today?"

"Yes. We spoke a short while ago. I have reassured her. We both appreciate your interest and concern but it is misdirected in this instance. Judith is in no danger whatever. If you will send me a bill, I will see that you are adequately compensated for your time."

I could not believe my ears.

I asked him, "Are you aware that five members of Judith's cast were murdered last night?"

He told me, "I have spoken at some length with the sheriff of San Bernardino county. Yes, I am quite aware of the tragedies. But the culprits are behind bars and I have been assured that my daughter is in no danger whatever."

I said, "Your Honor . . . the men who are behind bars

are two deputy marshals who are working out of your court. I can't believe that—"

"Yes, I know all about that."

"Then you'd best pull your head out of your ass, sir, and—"

"Mr. Copp! I appreciate what you're trying to do but I must make it quite clear to you that your interference is neither needed, warranted nor desired. The matter is totally in hand. Do you understand me?"

I replied, "No, Your Honor, I guess I just don't understand. If all the culprits are behind bars, how come there's an APB out on me at this very moment?"

"From San Bernardino county?"

"Yes, sir."

"I'll take care of that."

"You will?"

"Of course I will. Now go home, Mr. Copp, get some well-deserved rest, and send me a bill when you've figured it all out."

At that, the judge hung up on me. He hadn't been exactly hostile. Call it benignly authoritative.

Send him a bill, eh?

For what? Figure it all out? Okay. How about ten grand apiece for two false arrests? Another ten grand for assault on my body, say five grand each for two gun ambushes, twenty grand for false imprisonment and a hundred grand for involving me with the tragic remains of five viciously murdered kids.

Send the judge a bill?

I gazed around at Judith's bedroom, saw a vision of her kneeling naked on the big bed, shaking her butt and taunting me with hotly demanding eyes.

I couldn't send the judge a bill.

I'd already taken it out in trade with the judge's daughter—or should I put that on the bill too?

I was steamed, right.

More than that, though, I was downright scared. Then suddenly all that melted under the realization of what that conversation with the judge had really meant.

He'd made his peace.

Judge White had sold out to the mob.

CHAPTER 20

OKAY. I WAS home clean, you could say. Judith was in no danger. I was in no danger and everything was being squared with the cops. Five people were dead but . . . what the hell?—you can't bring them back and I hadn't heard anyone begging me to make justice triumphant.

So why couldn't I let it go? Hell I don't know why, except to say that I never could let go of things that seemed unfinished. In five years at SFPD I couldn't let go, five years at LAPD and another five with L.A. county—to "let go" was something I'd never learned how to do, never learned the politics of law enforcement. It was my "big flaw," as a captain at LAPD once told me. "If you want to advance in this department, Joe, you've got to learn to be more resilient."

Guess I always figured that resiliency, in police work, meant the art of compromise and I never had a lot of respect for that idea. Let the lawyers compromise and make their deals, that's what they're best at anyway, but *after* the cop on the case has established all the facts and tied the thing into a neat bundle for prosecution. A cop can't be resilient and be a good cop. He can't look the other way or shrug it off or deliberately ignore the loose ends of a case, not if he wants to respect himself.

If you can't buy that then I guess I can't explain why I was in a quiet rage following that conversation with Judge White. Wasn't mad at the judge, didn't even disrespect him for his attitude in the matter. I think I would have disrespected him more for going the other way to an extreme and proceeding against DiCenza in cold disregard for his daughter's fate. Actually, I felt a great relief for Judith's sake and, sure, for my own sake too, but something underneath was nettling the hell out of me and I couldn't shake it off.

I drank half a pot of Gertie's coffee and raided the refrigerator, made several more phone calls from Judith's telephone, and still I couldn't shake it off.

One of those calls was to my own lawyer. Doesn't cost me anything to call a lawyer. We have a barter deal. I help him and he helps me when the need is there, no bills are rendered, and he is one of the sharpest criminal lawyers in the area. We are also friends and I'd trust the guy with my life—I've done so on several occasions.

I asked my lawyer, "Tell me all you think you know about Judge White."

"District Court judge?"

"That's the one."

"He's fair. Tough, but fair. Brilliant man, actually. I've never argued before him in federal court but many times in Superior Court. What do you want to know?"

"Is he honest?"

"Never heard anything to the contrary. Appointed to the

federal bench several years ago without any opposition that I know about. No, he's clean as far as I know."

"Political debts?"

"Come on, Joe, every judge has political debts. But I doubt that anyone owns him, if that's what you mean."

"He's been on a tough case."

"Immensely. Lots of media attention."

"What's the courthouse gossip on that one?"

"DiCenza will go down."

"How hard?"

"With White on the bench, plenty hard. We're talking maybe fifty years."

"Which would be equal to a life sentence."

"In his case, yes. He's sixty now and he's sick."

"How sick?"

"He's diabetic. High blood pressure. Various circulatory disorders. Sick enough."

I reminded him, "There have been rumors of a deal. What about that?"

"There are always rumors of a deal in a case like this one, Joe. DiCenza could nail a lot of people. I think maybe they're just hopeful rumors this time. Judge White has never been particularly amenable to deals in his court. That's why they call him a hanging judge. Do you have an interest in this one?"

I said, "Maybe."

"Anything to do with uh . . . ?"

He was referring to my kidnap-rape thing.

I said, "Maybe."

"You're still clean on that one though?"

"Yeah."

"That was weird."

I told him, "It was only the begininng of weird. Tell me something. How weird would it be for you if Judge White should turn totally around on the DiCenza thing?"

"Meaning?"

"Meaning a deal with DiCenza."

The line was silent for a moment while my expert thought about it, then he told me, "Let me tell you why I do not believe that will happen, Joe. Too many nervous people on the party line."

"I didn't get that."

"There are too many people stretching all the way from L.A. to Sacramento and on to Washington who do not want to see a deal made with DiCenza. If DiCenza talks, a lot of people will fall with him, a lot of politically important people. Those people want DiCenza to take it like a man, to go down all by himself—and that will not happen if his lawyers are able to strike a deal for a light sentence. The pressure on Judge White to strike a deal is not coming from his side of the political aisle. Do you get my meaning?"

"The pressure that counts," I replied, "is against the deal."

"That's right."

"So why couldn't he make everybody happy and just give the guy a light sentence without a deal?"

"Too late for that. The new federal judicial guidelines are in effect in this case and the jury found the man guilty on all counts. A mandatory minimum sentence is involved there, and even that minimum would be like a life sentence for DiCenza. He cannot buy any time at all. The only deal that would mean anything for DiCenza would be a release on probation. Short of a major gesture on the defendant's part to cooperate with the prosecution in other cases, Judge White's hands are tied. He has to observe the guidelines. Besides . . ."

"Besides what?"

"There's been talk . . ."

"About what?"

"Well . . . speculation . . . that Judge White is next in line for a Supreme Court nomination."

I said, "We're talking damned heavy politics now."

"That's what we're talking," my lawyer agreed. "So I would have to say, in answer to your question, that I would regard it as intensely weird if Judge White were to step out of character in any way right now. There's a lot more at stake here, Joe, than the fate of a sick old mobster."

That was what I thought too. I thanked my friend the lawyer for his counsel and immediately called another friend. This one works for L.A. county and we'd once been partners. He now mans a desk at one of the many sheriff's substations scattered about the county, and I'm not going to give you his name either.

He exploded into my ear. "Joe! What the hell is going on with you?"

I replied, "Too much, pal, much too much. Do you have an APB on me?"

"Had one, yeah, out of San Bernardino, but I just got a cancellation a minute ago. What the hell is it?"

"Little misunderstanding," I told him. "That's all I wanted. Thanks. Go back to your knitting."

He said, as he hung up, "Beats the hell out of what you're doing these days, buddy."

Maybe it did.

I tried to call Art Lahey and was told that he was off duty.

Off duty? Lahey was never off duty.

I wandered about the big house and looked at the family photos that were scattered around. Judith was there from infancy, as a young ballerina of eight or nine, as a successful actress on many stages around the world, as a thoughtful young director brooding over her dinner theater.

The late Mrs. White was everywhere too, beautiful woman with that same excited quality in the eyes as the daughter—and she'd been an actress too, apparently a quite successful actress.

And the judge was there. Impressive, even as a young man. Tall and straight and handsome—and I could see Judith in his eyes too. The judge that commanded me, though, was a recent one—strong jaw, piercing eyes, very handsome guy in his mid-fifties, I'd say, with thick and wavy black hair, touch of silver at each temple—the kind of man you'd like to see wearing the robe of an Associate Justice of the United States Supreme Court.

I asked him, "What have you gotten yourself into here, Judge?"

Then I went out to find the answer to that question.

CHAPTER 21

I STOPPED OFF at my place and strapped on some hardware, took some cash out of my safe, stashed a riot gun in the trunk of my car and went on to Studio City. That's on the back side of the Hollywood hills in the area referred to around there as simply "the valley," as though the San Fernando were the only valley around. It's not, of course, but it does contain a large chunk of the L.A. population and many of the Hollywood people live in that valley, so it's an understandable conceit.

Actually, that valley has become almost as slummy as Hollywood itself but that's neither here nor there because the entire crazy patchwork quilt that is the Los Angeles basin is getting that way, with no "safe harbors" that far removed from urban decay and inner-city problems. Drugs and gangs and drive-by shootings, prostitutes and pimps and "decadent" lifestyles are everywhere the freeways travel these days. I'd worked in just about all those neighborhoods for more than ten years and I'd seen most of it happen.

But I wasn't looking for the urban decay of Studio City. I went on up Coldwater Canyon into the hills overlooking the valley in the expectation that I would find the decaying remains of a small criminal empire—its headquarters, that is—still clinging tenaciously to the earth despite all the slides and fires and other natural inconveniences that plague the cliffdwellers in that area.

The other side of the hill from that point is not Hollywood but Beverly Hills. The homes near the top are therefore very affluent diggings, and the denizens pay dearly for their perch. A hundred years ago no one in his right mind would have dreamed of building a house on the near vertical slopes of that twisting canyon, but then came architects and engineers with daring ideas and improved technologies that allowed them to suspend cantilevered mansions in thin air for adventurous and well-heeled patrons who liked the idea of living dangerously above it all. Dangerously because despite the best laid plans of engineer and architect, one or two of those architectural marvels continue to slide down the walls of Coldwater Canyon at some point during each rainy season.

Dangerously, also, because even in the best of times the decks of many of those homes are floating several hundred feet above the floor of the canyon; one step or stagger in the wrong direction during a patio party could be the last mistake you'd ever make.

The location I sought was one such as those.

I hadn't been there in many years, since I was a detective working vice out of the Hollywood division, still a bit wet behind the ears and not nearly as streetwise as I thought I was. I had not gone there in an official capacity but as an invited guest at a big party. Never mind, I hadn't gone to party but to satisfy a curiosity about the host, a kid fresh out of Columbia who'd just moved out from New York and opened a strip joint on my beat. He'd also been calling himself a "producer" and his name was DiCenza—not Vincent but James, Vincent's kid—so I had an idea of what he was producing.

He'd been in town only a couple of months when I went to the party but already he'd become a fixture in the local erotica and I just wanted a look at the guy up close.

I had thought he was just another punk with big ideas. Without his old man backing him he would have been working an adding machine in some back room somewhere. Actually I was surprised when I met the guy. He seemed pretty sharp and very self-assured but also the guy had a certain charm, nice smile, good eyes, and he was steady enough to have earned a degree in business from Columbia. As far as I could determine at the time he'd been running a clean operation strictly within the law, more so than a lot of the sex peddlers in this town that sex built.

I never had Victorian ideas about sex. Never even saw anything wrong with prostitution *per se* as long as it was kept *per se*, a gal and her John getting together in an honest contract with no outside interests involved. As for the strip joints—what the hell?—if the guys didn't mind watered drinks and were satisfied to look and not touch, if nobody was getting ripped off and the girls weren't being unfairly exploited—why the hell should I care? Strip joints are within the law and my job was only to enforce the law, not to pass moral judgment on human nature.

So I'd gone to Jimmy DiCenza's party out of curiosity as to why I'd been invited in the first place.

And it was quite a party.

About thirty sexy girls, about ten guys. The guys were all cops. The girls were all willing. And there was a promise of more parties with a constantly rotating female guest list. And of course there was the pitch. Nothing blatant, nothing actually incriminating, but a pitch nonetheless. Jimmy was expanding, opening a string of joints—even a couple of pizza parlors with topless waitresses—and Jimmy needed a security force to make sure that everyone behaved themselves.

So would any of us happen to know any good cops, any real good honest and reliable and dependable cops, who would like to moonlight as Jimmy's security force? The pay was excellent and nothing rigorous would be involved, they could set their own hours and punch their own clocks, just look in every now and then and make sure everything was okay. Would we know any like that?

Well, all ten of us were vice cops.

I'm sad to say that some of those guys went for it. I didn't, not because I'm holy but because I knew what was going down—and because to accept the first dollar from guys like these is to sell your soul to the devil. They own you from that point, and I don't like being owned.

I'd seen Jimmy around, over the years. I'd known that he'd gone from strip joints to porno flicks and call girls and whatever else he could dip his wick into without inciting too much heat in the law—and I'd known that he'd had protection all those years.

But I had not expected that he would remember me.

I handed my card to a spacey-eyed sexpot at the door and told her, "Tell Jimmy he needs to see me."

I didn't even know at the time if Jimmy lived there anymore, but I was soon ushered inside and escorted through the mansion and out onto the dizzying deck that

I still remembered in all its vertiginous splendor with its potted trees and tropical plants, hot tub and small pool, maybe a quarter of an acre complete with lawn sodded onto floating concrete several hundred feet above terra firma.

Six technically naked space cadets were adorning the sunning boards beside the pool and Jimmy was holding court beneath a nearby umbrella table with three Oriental gentlemen. The years had been kind to him physically, didn't look much older than the first time I'd seen him—at first appearance, a good-looking young businessman with the world by the tail. That impression would change.

He grabbed my hand and shook it warmly, then introduced me to his other guests. They had Japanese names which I don't remember and they were visiting from Tokyo.

It seemed that they were just leaving.

I was made comfortable with a drink while Jimmy walked the others out, and I was getting a lot of smiles and silent invitations from the sunning boards during his absence. But I cooled it and sipped my drink and waited.

Jimmy was looking very tired when he returned to the table. And all the warmth was gone. He asked me, "What do you want? Things getting tough out there in the big wild world all by yourself alone?"

I told him, "I've always been all by myself alone and so have you, pal, so have we all. What's with the Japanese?"

"Strictly legit," he replied. "It's been that way for a long time. I don't fuck around with crazy stuff anymore. Do you?"

"Never did," I told him. "What kind of legit?"

He lit a cigarette and told me around the smoke, "Not that it's any of your business but I'm a packager and promoter now."

"You always were. What are you packaging and promoting now?"

He leaned back in his chair and regarded me with speculative eyes for a long moment, then he chuckled and said, "Some people never change. Joe, you never will. You were an asshole when I first met you and you're an asshole now. Why all the sudden interest in Jimmy DiCenza?"

I told him, "Your old man is going down hard."

Those dark eyes flared and went very flat, he sucked hard on the cigarette. "Says who?"

"I have an inside line."

"Then you'd better check the connection. I talked to him not an hour ago. He's going to walk."

I said, "Oh. Well I'm glad to hear that."

"Are you?"

"Sure I am. I've always been kind to the elderly. I see no sense in sending a dying man to jail."

Jimmy said, "He's not dying."

"That's not the way I hear it. But I'm not worried about Vin, Jimmy. I worry about you."

"Why would you do that?"

I looked around, asked him, "Is this your palace guard? Are they going to protect you with their bare assess, Jimmy?"

"I don't need protection," he replied in a hollow voice.

I unholstered my pistol and placed it on the table between us. "That's not what I hear."

Jimmy was ignoring the pistol. "What do you hear?"

"Your old man is going down hard. Forget anything else

you heard. He's going down hard, and the only way he can prevent that is to send a bunch of other people down in his place. These are very powerful people, Jimmy. They don't want to go down."

"Why are you telling me this?"

"For old times sake."

He looked at the gun and then quickly back at me. "What old times? You never wanted to dance with me, Joe. Why now?"

I sighed heavily and told him, "Maybe I'm getting tired of dancing alone. I'm into this thing to my eyebrows."

"What thing?"

"This DiCenza thing, dammit. I've been shot at, beat up, set up, thrown into jail—I'm tired of it. I want it to stop."

He was looking at me as though he were an artist measuring me for a canvas. "I don't know what the hell you're talking about, Joe."

"What are you packaging and producing these days, Jimmy?"

He worked at the cigarette for a moment, gave me several fast glances, looked into the sky just past my head and said, "I'm in show business. Legit show business. I'm not shooting at or beating up anyone, and I wouldn't know how to set anyone up for jail. Just because I'm Vincent DiCenza's kid doesn't mean that I am heir-apparent to anything or that I want to be. I've never really been in the rackets and never wanted to be. Vin has always respected that. In fact, he has always preferred it that way. He sent me to Columbia to keep me out of the rackets. So I don't know what you're talking about."

"You're exporting shows to Japan?"

"Among other places, yes."

I had a sudden inspiration; asked him, "Do you have any connection with the East Foothills Dinner Theater?"

He looked me straight back with a curled smile. "So that's it."

"You've heard?"

"Sure I've heard. Did Judy send you?"

Judy, yet. I guess my own lips curled on that one. "Not that she knows," I replied, trying to keep the disappointment out of my voice. "What's the connection?"

"What's your interest?"

"I'm trying to keep alive. Maybe you should be trying that too. A lot of people already tried too late and they are running out of morgue space out my way."

Jimmy stared at me for a long moment, then he sighed and put his feet up, took a pull at his drink, finally said to me, "I've known Judy a long time. She used to work for me, sort of. Now sometimes she sends me talent."

"What kind of talent?"

"Not your kind," he replied smilingly. "How'd you get into this?"

"What kind of talent?" I repeated.

He kept on smiling. "Singers, dancers, that kind of talent. I told you I'm legit."

I asked him, "Are you the mysterious producer who was going to package *La Mancha* for a national tour?"

Jimmy DiCenza laughed at that. When he was done laughing he looked over at the sunning boards and invited me with the eyes to do the same. "I don't package national, I package international, and I don't waste my time with boy shows, they wouldn't play on my circuits."

"Boy shows?"

"Not enough female involvement in *La Mancha,*" he explained. "It's a boy's stage, not a girl's. American entertainers have gotten very big in Japan. But they want girls, see. Long-legged, big-busted Caucasian girls." His eyes jerked again toward the sun boards. "Like these."

"So you're still packaging flesh shows."

He frowned at me. "Somebody pass a law against that?"

I shrugged and told him, "Depends on what's in the package. I'm no moralist, Jimmy, you know that. I didn't come here to shame you."

"So why did you come?"

I retrieved my pistol and holstered it, told him, "Maybe I came to save your life. Vin is going down hard unless he can find some replacements. That means people close to him in business."

Jimmy DiCenza was getting pissed at me. His lips were curled in a snarl as he said, "You trying to tell me that my own father would sell me down?"

"Are you in business with Japanese politicians, Jimmy?"

His eyes recoiled a bit on that one. "Get out of here," he said in a flat voice. "And don't ever come back."

"Does Vin know that you're connected with the judge's daughter?"

That one brought a solid reaction. His feet came down and he jerked forward in his chair. "Jesus! I never made it! Never put it—never realized—Jesus!" The Don's son was beginning to look old and tired.

I was suddenly feeling very old and tired myself. I got to my feet and walked away, then turned back for another look. The guy hadn't moved, hadn't changed his face. I said, "Everyone's dying, Jimmy. Why?"

Then I let myself out and went slowly back down the mountain, down into the valley of despair and utter darkness.

It was a long way down.

CHAPTER 22

HELL, I DIDN'T know what I had now. There are times when too much equals nothing, when the puzzle gets so broken and jumbled that the sheer mass of it defeats you. That is about where I was at when I left Jimmy DiCenza. I was in a whirl. And why not? Every piece I touched fragmented into several other pieces and the puzzle was breaking apart, not coming together to form a true picture of anything.

I didn't even know if Jimmy had been straight with me. Why should he be? On the other hand, he'd popped me right in the snoot with Judy. So why shouldn't he be? And no way could he have been faking the sudden realization that Judy White was Judge White's daughter.

I had left a frightened man behind.

Granted, I'd been trying to frighten him—but why had it worked? What was he frightened of?

I was inclined to believe Jimmy's claim that he was in no bigtime involvements with his old man. I'd seen enough over the years to make that sound credible, and in fact it had been more or less common knowledge for years that Vin DiCenza had gone to pains to keep his kid at a distance from the crime families and their internecine disputes. He'd bankrolled the kid, sure, in various quasi-legal pursuits, and he'd extended his own protective umbrella several times to keep the kid out of trouble with the law, but that was about the extent of it in any way that I'd ever heard about.

Like I said earlier, Jimmy DiCenza had kept himself pretty clean through the years.

But it was begging too much to chalk it all to coincidence that the kid apparently had a longterm relationship of one kind or another with the daughter of the judge who now held the old man's fate in his judicial hands.

I mean, okay, coincidences do happen but . . .

I needed to know a lot more than I thought I knew about the DiCenzas and the Whites.

So okay, I knew where to start on that . . . but did I really want to start there? Did I want to confront Judith with this new information and challenge her to come clean with me?

Not yet, no.

So I went for the other White.

I'd filched the judge's West L.A. address from an address book while I was at Judith's place but with no particular plan at the time to do anything with it. You don't just barge in on a federal judge, especially under the circumstances, but those very circumstances now seemed to demand it.

By now it was seven o'clock and the day was trying to drag me down. I pulled through a McDonald's and choked down a Big Mac enroute to the highrise section of Wilshire in West L.A., just to keep my motor running and the juices circulating. That particular strip of L.A. looks more East Coast than West, I think maybe because East Coast money built it and inhabited it, sort of like a fashionable neighborhood in Manhattan. I think they're all crazy, myself, to put up those kind of residential buildings in earthquake country, state-of-the-art engineering notwithstanding, but what do I know?

I could see a bigshot lawyer inhabiting one of those million-dollar condos, though. Not necessarily a judge of any kind who depends on his salary for lifestyle—but again, what do I know?

At least this judge was not living in a penthouse. He had a corner of the twenty-first floor in a very swank building but the apartment is no great shakes. I know that because I let myself inside and snooped around just for feel. It felt more like chambers than home, the same leather and dark wood and books, books, books. One bedroom, very plain, queensize bed, TV, VCR, a locked cabinet of tapes. Small study, small desk littered with papers and legal tablets, portable typewriter, snubnosed pistol in the top drawer—loaded—not much else.

Small bar off the living room—the usual liquids in fancy bottles—and I finished the tour more puzzled about the man than when I'd come in. There was no signature here, no statement, no proclamation of self: "This is me. It's what I'm like, what I do, who I am."

It occurred to me then that I'd found the same lack in the mansion at San Antonio Heights. I'd chalked it up to the idea that it was more a museum than someone's home—and I got that same idea here at the highrise condo.

I went a step farther in my investigation and became even more puzzled. There was a walk-in closet in the bedroom. One side contained men's suits, shirts, shoes, the usual stuff. The other side was devoted to dresses, furs, the usual feminine stuff.

So I tried the bathroom.

It was a his and hers arrangement, with all the usual stuff for both. ·

It seemed that the judge had a live-in girlfriend.

And I wondered if Judith knew about that.

Federal judges get their jobs by presidential appointment. This means that they are political animals, like it or not, the same as all judges everywhere in this country—and I always figured that the system works against the electorate, you and me, in that mainly what we get as judges are people who do not do too well as lawyers.

Last time I noticed, District Court judges get an annual salary of under ninety thousand dollars. That may seem like a lot if you're only getting twenty or thirty but even ninety a year does not buy that much these days.

A rookie cop at LAPD fresh out of the academy draws down about thirty-three as a minimum, with some closer to forty. I've known married cops—two cops married to each other, I mean—with a combined salary of more than ninety a year. So what hotshot lawyer with all those years of struggling education behind him would want to settle for a judgeship?

See?—it's an inverse system in which the cream does not rise to the top but lurks along the bottom. You could argue, and I've done it myself, that many lawyers are scumbags anyway who have no respect whatever for the law except as they can twist it around to their own advantage, so the system actually works better than it would appear—that the best lawyers can't be measured by their incomes but by their love of the law and a strong desire to serve same, and that these are the ones who are drawn toward the political arena and public service.

Sure, I've argued that. But I haven't always convinced myself that it is true. I've seen scumbags on the bench too, and of course our whole political process in this country has been taken over by the lawyers. It is rare to find a congressman or a legislator or even a city councilman who did not begin with a law degree. What makes a judge that different from any of those? He has had to kiss somebody's ass to get that job, probably a horde of somebodies.

So what was I thinking about here?

I was thinking that politicians as a class are as dishonest and self-serving as any occupational group in the country, probably more so, and that every judge, even a highly respected federal judge, is a politician. They're all of a stripe, and pardon my cynicism but you'd have to search high and low to find a political animal who is scrupulously honest and the sole owner of his own soul.

Sometimes I get mad that I have to think that way. Shouldn't be that way. But I felt that way because I had spent fifteen years watching these guys enrich themselves at the public's expense and I know how the games are played.

I knew also that ninety thou a year does not buy the lifestyle that Judge White enjoys.

So what was I thinking?

Tell me what I was thinking. I was staggering about in the dark, sure, but I wasn't totally blind yet. I knew, too, that it was time to get back to the basics of police work, and I knew where to start again.

I made another call enroute to my own valley but this time I didn't pick a lock, I just kicked the door open and went on in.

It was a crack house on the east side and I instantly had

four Chicanos brandishing knives in my face but I pushed on through that and went into the back room where I expected to find Cholly Esteves, head of a neighborhood gang coalition and reputedly "the man to see" for drug distributorships east of L.A.

I found him okay, seated at a big dining room table covered with stacks of old bills and running a tabulation on a small portable computer. I found also a dozen or so other people in various states of dress and undress, men and women, bombed out of their heads and just sitting around grinning vacantly at one another.

Never figured out the appeal of that shit.

I mean, is this paradise?—this mindless, careless, sexless, meaningless zombied state? Is this something to spend your entire life pursuing, something for which you'd betray parents and children, employers and employees, friends and neighbors and ultimately the world? Is it? Before a kid can take his first hit, he needs to see inside one of these places and get a good look at the zombies. I think he'd change his mind, damned quick.

Esteves looked up at me with a frown and growled, "Whattaya mean coming in here that way? Go back outside and try it again."

I said, "Get screwed, Cholly, if you're not afraid your dick will fall off into the crack."

"You want one of the women?"

"I wouldn't do it with your dick, pal," I told him. "I wouldn't wearing a wetsuit and twenty condoms."

"Okay, you made your point," he said, grinning. "You don't like my women."

I said, "I don't like a damned thing I see here. Not even you—and that goes back a long time, Cholly."

"So why'd you bring your stiff ass in here?"

"Couldn't help myself. And you owe me."

The big Mexican laughed and scooted his chair back to face me full on. "How many more times do I have to pay you, man?"

"As often as I'm in need," I told him.

"Uh huh."

I said, "Okay, we'll settle the tab in full this time."

"What do you need?"

"Who's supplying the East Foothills area?"

"Go to hell," he said.

"Someone out that way made a big buy earlier this week. I have to know who."

"*Have* to know?"

"That's what I said."

He glared at me for a moment then reached for the telephone. "Which brand of passion?"

"Coke. Pretty white powders."

"That's west side passion," he grunted. "People out here prefer the rocks."

"Makes your little task all that easier," I suggested. "I really need it, Cholly."

"Okay." His hand was hovering above the telephone. "But then you owe me."

I said, "Let's see what you score, first."

He made the call, rattled off a long question in Spanish and received a long rattle in reply, put his hand over the transmitter and turned to me with a crooked smile. "How much it gonna be worth to you, man?"

I replied with another crooked smile. "A promise that you'll never see my stiff ass around here again."

"Hey, you got the wrong idea, Joe. It's not that I don't

like to see you. But you always insult my women and you make me feel bad. I want you to fuck one of my women, man."

"You want to watch, Cholly?"

He laughed, and then the telephone receiver rattled some more. He rattled back, looking at me all the while, then said to me, "He don't handle much powder over there, like I said. No big guys. But he's been delivering a bag a night for the past few weeks to the same place."

"What place is that?"

Another exchange across the telephone, then: "You know that stage show at that hotel out there?"

"Dinner theater," I said tightly.

"Sure, that's the one."

"Stage door delivery?"

Cholly put the question to the telephone then relayed the answer to me. "Just outside. She meets him in the parking lot."

"She?"

"Classy looking Anglo woman." Cholly laughed. "Probably the kind you'd fuck while I watched. But she's got a hundred dollar a night nose just the same."

"Blonde or brunette?"

Another telephone rattle, then: "He don't know, man. She always has this, uh, whattaya call shawl thing wrapped around her head."

"Spanish shawl."

"Yeah, yeah, like that."

Yeah, sure, like the women of La Mancha wear.

I thanked the druglord of the east side and went away from there.

Hundred dollar a night nose, maybe.

Then again, maybe it was just another weave in the web that had been building since at least two weeks earlier when someone walked into my gym with a Polaroid camera and snapped me in the buff. Maybe the hundred dollar a night buy was no more than a cautious stockpiling of stage props being assembled for a one night stand starring none other than the Copp for Hire.

How had Susan Baker put it? I wouldn't follow the script?

I knew what I had to do. I had to find that script.

CHAPTER 23

I HAD NOT forgotten the Minnesota connection either and I was resolved to explore that side of the web at the first opportunity. That is partly why I went on to the theater that evening, but also I wanted words with the judge's daughter and we sort of had a date anyway for after the show.

I had not expected to run into Art Lahey there, though. I guess he must have been sitting outside waiting for me to show because he came in almost on my heels and joined me at the darkened back wall of the theater. I'd arrived near the end of Act II in the middle of Lunceford's "Impossible Dream" number. I thought the guy was damned good. In fact, I think he was better than the guy he'd been understudying, more fire in the eyes or something and a bit more feeling in the voice, but what do I know.

I said as much to Lahey when he came alongside and he jumped me immediately. "Thought you hadn't seen Craig Maan in the role. You told me he cut out before the curtain went up."

"That time, yeah," I agreed. "But I saw the show awhile back."

"You didn't tell me that."

"Didn't think it would be important to tell you that."

"I guess there are a lot of things not important enough to tell me," he gibed.

The curtain came down for intermission at that point. The applause from the audience was enthusiastic but many of the oldsters were already out of their chairs and moving toward the rest rooms. Lahey took my elbow and steered me outside.

He lit a cigarette so I did one too and we strolled on across the patio for another thirty feet or so before Lahey spoke again. "Just so you'll know where we stand," he told me in a quietly sober voice, "I'm off the case."

I said, "Congratulations. But why?"

"I'm on suspension," he growled.

"For what?"

"Insubordination, threatening a superior, how many more do you want?"

"That'll do," I told him. "Welcome to the club. One of those too many is what drove me into the private sector. So what are you looking for now?—absolution?"

Lahey took a seat on a bench and grinned up at me as he said, "To tell the truth, I came down here with half the intention of kicking your teeth in. But that would be like kicking the whipped dog, wouldn't it. I watched you walk in there awhile ago and all the anger melted. You're as fucked up as I am, aren't you."

I sat down beside him, took a deep breath and let it all out, told him with no wind at all behind it, "I was set up coming into this thing, Art. You were not. So maybe you should tell me what has been going down here."

He said, "All I know for sure is that your friends Dobbs

and Harney were all ready to be nailed to the wall and I had the hammer. My boss took the hammer out of my hand . . . and I guess I took too much exception to that. Anyway, there is no case now. Your feds were released on a habeas corpus handed down by the Central District Court of California and so was a locker full of evidence."

I coughed on my cigarette, gave him a long hard scrutiny, then asked, "What evidence?"

"The clothing that Craig Maan wore out of here last night, bloodstained, and a video cassette that shows Dobbs and Harney busting into the second apartment."

I dropped the cigarette and ground it into the flagstones under my foot. I was very surprised at how calm I felt. "Where'd you find the clothing?"

"In their room here at the hotel."

"Who's room?"

"Larry Dobbs and Jack Harney. They've been registered here for the past two weeks. You didn't know that?"

I shook my head. "Guess I thought—I've been flat on my ass, Art. These people have had me chasing my own shadow. I'm ashamed to say that but it's true. What's that about a video tape? The one that was . . . ?"

"Yeah. It was a new tape, had only about twenty minutes recording time on it. Shows all the victims except the first one and shows them all alive and well and having fun. Then the camera pans to show your feds breaking through the door, this Elaine Suzanne in tow, and an abrupt end to the recording."

"That was supposed to be me," I declared in a hollow voice.

"What do you mean?"

"The way it was scripted. Elaine was supposed to have

taken me there. Instead, she took me to the other apartment. I don't know why unless she just got confused and blew it. And it knocked her out to see Craig sitting there with his throat slashed. That wasn't in the script."

"What's this script?"

"I talked to Susan Baker today at the hospital, after they moved her from the security ward. She let something slip but then caught herself and clammed up. Said enough though to give me the idea that some big plan came to fruition up there last night. I think it was some kind of a scam, but it backfired on them." I gave the cop a long, hard look. "Hate to tell you this, pal, but I think you went down for nothing. I don't think Dobbs and Harney did that to those kids."

"Yeah, so you said already," Lahey replied sourly. "But I didn't go down for nothing. I went down for a principle. Five people were viciously murdered in my jurisdiction last night. Whether those two did it or not—and I was only about fifty-one percent convinced that they did—I think those guys know who did it. If I could have kept the pressure on them, the truth would have come out sooner or later. Now I have the feeling that we'll never know."

I asked, "That the same reason you came after me?"

"Something like that, yeah," he replied soberly.

"At fifty-one percent?"

Lahey sighed. "It would've been worth it at ten percent."

"For you, maybe," I growled. "How the hell am I supposed to make a living if you guys keep coming at me on a ten percent hunch?"

He said, "It was more than a hunch, Joe. I had the snapshot. I had your prior involvement with the victim right out in public. I had the most ridiculous God damned story any P.I. ever told and not a shadow of a client. I had—"

"I explained that."

"That's what I mean by ridiculous. Do you have a client?"

"Two," I said. "It turns out that Susan Baker was my client. I returned her retainer today. Then there's a guy in Minnesota, this Johansen. Did I tell you that he's a judge?"

Lahey showed me a spooky look and replied, "Did I tell you that Craig Maan's real name is Johansen?"

Well, that stopped me, but only for half a breath. "No, I thought so too at first because I had this photo . . . but there was a switch, see, and I don't have that worked out yet. Something in the script, maybe, but Johnny Lunceford is the real Johansen."

Lahey said, "No, that's not right. Lunceford's real name is Lunceford. Maan's real name is Johansen. I've got fingerprint identification to prove it. Also, Johansen has worked as a paid informer for the FBI. I've got that too, it's in the paperwork served by the District Court."

I said, "Now wait a minute, dammit . . ."

I'd suddenly become aware that a sweet little lady of about eighty was listening to our conversation with rapt attention. I don't know how long she'd been there but she gave me a smile of pure joy and said, "That is positively fascinating! Is it the next play?"

I looked at Lahey, looked back at the sweet little lady and told her, "Gosh, ma'am, I hope not."

But maybe it was.

CHAPTER 24

MAYBE I SHOULD remind you that at this point I was less than seventy-two hours into this case. I know that seems ridiculous because so much had happened but that is the way it went. So if you think I was being very stupid about some of the developments, you're probably right, I was stupid, but let's be fair about it: someone had gone to a lot of pains to make me that way and I had not had a lot of time to work through it. The thing had begun for me on a Wednesday morning at three A.M. and we were now into the Friday evening performance of *La Mancha*.

You might remember that on the very first day, Wednesday—when I really did not consider myself on the case—I'd been shot at and then set up for a false rap and thrown into jail. So we should not even count that day. I actually began working it as a case on Thursday morning and the whole thing blew up in my face that night. It had been gangbusters ever since, except for the idyllic interlude with Judith White on Friday morning, and even that was more dizzying than refreshing, so why the hell shouldn't I be stupid?

So okay, I was stupid. But at least I knew at the time

that I was stupid and I was struggling like hell to smarten up.

Lahey did not go back inside with me for the final act that night. Suspended or not, he still had a very active interest in the case and he had a lead that he wanted to follow. Didn't want to tell me what it was but he did promise to keep me informed of developments. I promised him the same, although I had not told him everything I'd learned that day—but that's okay, because he had not told me everything either.

I went on back inside and Lahey went toward his car.

I have to say that the makeshift cast put on an inspired performance that evening. The final curtain brought the house down and it took three curtain calls to quiet the crowd. Lunceford had been spectacular in the title role and all the players had seemed to reach into their depths to really pull the thing together. It was essentially the same cast that had performed on Thursday, but this was the first performance after they'd learned of the deaths of their five fellow players—and they made it memorable.

I spoke to Lunceford backstage for the first time a few minutes folowing the final curtain call but he already knew who I was. Everyone was milling around and congratulating one another but it was a subdued group, not a joyous one. I tried to respect that mood, told Lunceford that it was very important that I talk with him before he went home that evening.

He seemed like a nice kid, very direct and cooperative, told me that he had to go straight to the hotel lounge as soon as he could get out of the makeup and stage clothes. "I sit in with the band over there every Friday and

Saturday," he explained, "but I only do a couple of numbers. If you'd like to meet me over there . . "

I told him I would like to do that, then I went looking for Judith, found her standing outside the women's dressing room. She gave me a pretty smile and asked, "How'd we do?"

"Knocked 'em dead, like you said," I replied. "How'd you know I was out there?"

"Saw you and Sergeant Lahey during intermission," she said. "You seemed very engrossed with each other so I . . ."

"No, we weren't all that . . ."

"Well I didn't want to . . ."

"No, you should have . . ."

She laughed suddenly and gave me a quick kiss on the lips. "Are we embarrassed or what? When a man and woman can't speak in complete sentences to each other, what does that mean? Are we . . . ?"

"I think maybe we . . ."

"But we've only known each other for . . ."

"Well sure, but . . ." I caught myself doing it again, chuckled and told her, "This could get dangerous. I'm meeting Johnny Lunceford in the lounge. Could you come over?"

"Daddy said he talked to you."

I said, "Yes. We had a good talk."

"So you're not worried about . . ."

"Well I don't know, Judy. Things are still a bit . . ."

"I mean, you wouldn't have to . . ."

"Oh no, I want to . . ."

She gave me a dazzling smile and said, "Stop that."

"You first," I said.

"In the lounge?"

I said, "Yes."

"I'll be there in about ten minutes. I have to . . ."

I don't know. What *does* it mean when a man and woman can't talk together coherently? Maybe all it means is that one or both of them are stupid.

But I didn't think so.

This hotel is one of those sprawling, Spanish hacienda types with many buildings scattered about, none more than two stories high, connected by flagstone pathways and buried in exotic trees and plants. There are several pools and I don't know how many restaurants, tennis courts and other recreational facilities, shops and offices that serve not only guests of the hotel but the general public as well.

The theater occupied one of those buildings near the outside of the complex. About a hundred yards away and connected by covered walkways and patios stood the building that housed a large restaurant and banquet facility serving fine, and expensive, continental cuisine. The hotel lounge, also, was in that building, separated from the restaurant by a foyer and heavy double doors.

It was a small lounge, as hotel lounges go. Room for maybe twenty at the bar and perhaps twenty tables in an intimate atmosphere grouped about a small stage and dance floor. The "band" was actually a duo—a big, goodlooking darkhaired guy at the keyboards and a pretty little blonde vocalist with Doris Day innocence and a seductive Streisand voice, very handsome couple. I thought it actually was a big band in there before I rounded the corner at the foyer and stepped inside. The guy was seated at one of these huge keyboard consoles and making bigband music complete with brass, string, and rhythm sections while the two of them were vocalizing a big production number from *Les Miserables*. They were sensational. I learned later that they called themselves *The Show Band* and all of their music was taken from hit Broadway musicals of the past and present.

It was nearly midnight and the place was still jammed. I stood by the bar while the band concluded their "I Have A Dream" number from *Miserables*, then I got a quick understanding of what Lunceford had meant by "sitting in." I guess he'd timed his entrance because he stepped through the doors at that moment. The little blonde announced through her microphone: "Oh good! Here's Johnny, everybody!" The guy did a fanfare with his keyboard. "Johnny, will you come up and do a number with us? Let's hear it for Johnny Lunceford, everybody—from the dinner theater next door, Johnny Lunceford."

The guy at the keyboards did a comical take-off on Ed McMahon as he shifted from fanfare to drumroll: "Heeeeeeeeeeeer's Johnny!" You could tell, this was a fun place with a more or less steady patronage by the surrounding community. Everyone seemed to know everyone else and they all loved their entertainers.

Lunceford leaped onto the stage to enthusiastic applause, cheers and whistling, hugged the blonde and wrung the keyboardist's hand, and the three went into a little huddle on stage while various patrons shouted out requests. I heard several different titles shouted out but "Impossible Dream" seemed to be the favorite, it seemed to be a standard for this guy. He was making a comically rueful face as the blonde dug out the music and placed it on the music stand for the keyboardist, there was a lot of goodnatured jawing back and forth between bandstand and audience while the musician set up his instrument, then a hush of anticipation fell with the downbeat.

This is one of those songs that starts sort of low-keyed and builds dramatically. The blonde was off the bandstand and moving toward the door as soon as the music began. Our eyes met as she brushed past me. Guess she thought she knew me. "Isn't he great?" she whispered. "Mind if I stand here? I appreciate it better from a distance."

I didn't mind, no. Beautiful gal, and I got an insight there. Talented people *dig* other talented people. I was watching her more than Lunceford as the number progressed and I liked what I saw there. It should be that way for everyone, I decided. A good carpenter should really *dig* another good carpenter, same for bookkeepers and bank tellers and corporate executives, same for cops. We should all *dig* excellence in others who do what we have chosen to do with our lives and not feel threatened by it. We should feel reassured by it.

The blonde glanced at me during a musical interlude and whispered, "Boy! Such power!"

I said, "Yeah. That's exactly what I was thinking about you and your partner. You should be in musical theater."

She wrinkled her nose and replied, "Can't afford it," then turned back to the stage as Lunceford began his fortissimo conclusion.

That was another insight, brought home to roost. Craig Maan had hinted at it during our conversation the day he died when he told me, "We work for carfare, not for limousines." Apparently lounge singers do better than that.

The number ended and the place went wild.

To "sit in" is to do it for free.

But I could tell by Johnny Lunceford's reaction to the applause that he was not doing it "for free." He was doing it for love, and at that moment he was indeed adored.

It should be that way for all of us, I decided, when we do well the things that we do.

Certainly we should not be killed for it.

CHAPTER 25

"THESE GUYS ARE the greatest," Lunceford told me in admiring tones, referring to the band. They'd taken a break after his number and a few patrons immediately left, as though waiting for that moment to quit the place, and that opened some tables. I'd taken one in a back corner and Lunceford had joined me there.

"Mack has been coaching me on the side, helping me with microphone technique and all that. You know it's a whole different ball game when you're in an intimate situation like this. It's like you're more than a singer, you're the host at a party, you have to command the room and you don't have a script to follow.

"If you can't do that then you can't work in a lounge, no matter how good your music is. So they're great, they're the best, and I owe them a lot. Janie's the best, the absolute best there is. If we weren't both married, I'd be in love with her. She and Mack are married. Isn't that great?

"What a great way to make a living, singing love songs with someone you truly love. They do casuals all over the place too, wedding receptions and all kind of private parties, they're together night and day, seven days and nights a week, and they're still in love. Isn't that great?

"That's what I'd like to do. But my wife can't sing. Well, I told her to take up the piano anyway. I mean we could do this, if she'd learn keyboards. She's not musical, though, not at all."

He peered sadly into his beer then took a long pull at it. I didn't know if he was running the jaw that way because he was nervous with me or if he always went on that way.

"I told Alfie we could do it, he wasn't that bad with keyboards—hell, we could fake it, with all the electronic help you can get these days. We could work up an act and Mack would help us find a gig, he's a great guy. But Alfie liked the big stage, he liked . . ."

I got a single word in. "Alfie?"

"You knew him as Craig Maan. That was a funny deal, I want you to know how that came about. Alfie had been into all kinds of dumb shit. I don't know—he was just too much of a romantic, I guess. Big dreams, big deals, always the big deals. We met in college. Both majoring in drama. His dad thought he was majoring in chemical engineering. Right there, see, he was already living a lie. I don't know how you can do that. I mean . . . that's just too much intrigue, I couldn't live that way.

"For Alfie it just seemed natural, the way to go. So—"

"What happened after college?"

"I was two years ahead of him. I graduated and came out here. I've been living a double life myself for the past two years—but on the up and up, see. Couldn't get any regular television or stage work so I had to take a job. I wanted to get married. Hell, I had to make a living. So I make my living during the day and I work toward the future at night. Maybe some day I'll make my living at night. I'd like that."

"You were telling me about this funny deal."

"I don't know, Alfie got into some kind of dumb shit after I graduated and came out here. From the University of Chicago, that's where we went to school. I guess he spent his whole junior year with one dumb thing after another. He dropped out in his senior year and showed up on my doorstep one day, said he didn't want anyone to know where he was.

"Now listen to this, this is really dumb. Alfie told me that he'd gotten involved with this older man, a gay man old enough to be his father, and that this gay man had been sponsoring him in a career—a showbiz career—but Alfie couldn't stand it any more, he had to get out of the relationship. But he owed this man a lot of money and the man didn't want to let him go. Alfie wanted to live incognito for awhile, he needed a job and he especially didn't want his father to know anything about his problems.

"Well, I've been working in dinner and community theater all the time I've been out here. Most of it is equity waiver so you don't make a lot of money but it's a good place to learn the ropes and improve yourself and maybe even get noticed by somebody who can help your career. There's a lot of that kind of work out here so you can work fairly steady if you don't mind bumping along from one small theater to another."

"And," I added, "If you don't mind working for carfare."

"That's exactly right. Alfie wasn't married, didn't have any bills to speak of—except to his gay friend—and pocket money was really all he needed for the time being. I had just auditioned for this production of *La Mancha* and landed the role as the Padre. This other guy, Greg Houston, landed the title role. Greg is older, he's done *La Mancha* all over the place, and he was even on Broadway years ago, briefly. Anyway, a few small roles were still open or at least questionable so I took Alfie in to see Judith.

"Well there was instant chemistry there. And Greg Houston had just called that very morning to say that he'd gotten a better offer from San Francisco and he'd like to bow out of *La Mancha*. The upshot of it all is that Alfie stepped into the title role two days before the show opened and he was like born for the part.

"Look, I'm not modest—I know I sing better than Alfie. Well, I've worked harder at it. But he like brought Miguel Cervantes to life on that stage. He was great, and everyone knew it. It's a great tragedy, and great loss that he was snatched away from us. Everyone loved Alfie, and I mean everyone."

"The funny deal," I prompted.

"Oh, yeah . . . I thought it was a gag, I mean it started out like a gag. Alfie wanted to be incognito. He auditioned as Craig Maan and he got the role as Craig Maan. Then he started telling people that *my* real name was Alfred Johansen. I thought, 'What the hell is this?'—but I went along with it and it got to be a real gag. I mean I even told stories about Alfie as though they were my stories—you know, college stuff and all that, stories about Alfie's father and all that. That's the way it got started. It was just a gag."

"Some gag," I commented. "It had a lot of people fooled."

"For a long time, yeah. This has been going on for about

three months. Then a few weeks ago he started this thing about the national tour. Now I knew that was bullshit. I knew it from the start. I mean, I didn't *know* that it was bullshit, he never told me that it was, but I just knew from the way it got started that it was another one of Alfie's dumb stunts."

I asked, "How did it start?"

"It started," Lunceford replied, "as a gag."

"How so?"

"These two new waiters started at the theater. Alfie turned white the first time he spotted them from the stage, and he pointed them out to me from backstage during intermission. He told me that they'd been looking for him and it looked like they'd finally caught up with him."

"This was Larry and Jack."

"That's right. He said they were private detectives hired by his old gay friend. Then later on that same night he told me that they'd brought a proposition to him. The old man wanted to give him a chance to settle his debts. He would bankroll—the old gay man—he would bankroll the show for a national tour if Alfie would agree to remain in the title role.

"Well, I thought that was bullshit. It sounded like bullshit to me. But he began repeating it around and the rest of the cast bought it. I guess when you've wanted something so bad for so long . . . and the other kids didn't know Alfie like I know Alfie. I knew it was bullshit but I never said anything. I should have. Especially when . . ."

"When what?"

"When he came up with this . . ."

"This what?"

"This dumb . . . plot, I guess. He called it insurance."

"Insurance for what?"

"To keep the old gay man in check, I guess. 'To keep him honest,' was the way Alfie put it. He wanted to involve the entire cast in the plot. We were all supposed to chip in a week's paycheck. We'd hire another private detective to protect him—him being Alfie—and Alfie would arrange the insurance."

"Why would Alfie need protection to do that?"

"This old gay man . . ."

"What about him?"

Lunceford chuckled. "Alfie told us he was a Mafia godfather. Can you imagine? A gay godfather?"

I chuckled, too, but not with humor. "Did Alfie ever name this gay godfather?"

"No. I never bothered to ask because I knew it was bullshit. And I was not about to contribute a week's pay for one of Alfie's gags. I have responsibilities, about to become a father. What it finally came down to was five people who bought into it, and—"

I said, "That would be Elaine, Susan and the three guys—Peterson, Sanchez and Stein."

Lunceford nodded his head soberly at each name. "Yes, may God bless. I thought they were all nuts to go along with that. But now I don't know. I guess it wasn't a gag. Five people are dead, aren't they."

"Five of six," I mused aloud. "Why do you suppose Susan was spared?"

"I guess she was just in the right place at the right time," Lunceford replied. "I don't know why, unless she just got lucky." He shivered. "It could have happened to me. What would have become of my wife and kid? Huh? I'm a bit pissed at Alfie, even though he's dead. He's responsible for all of that, him and his dumb shit."

"What was the script, Johnny?" I asked casually.

"What script?"

"The insurance script. What was the plan?"

He shook his head. "I don't know, didn't want to know. I was glad when you said you wanted to talk to me because I wanted that too. Just want you to know that I had nothing to do with any of it. Well, except one thing. I did . . ."

"You did what?"

"I was worried about maybe I *was* involved, that maybe Alfie had involved me without my knowing about it. So I . . . well, that's why I called Alfie's father."

"You're the one."

"I called him, yeah. I didn't want Alfie to know that I'd finked on him, but the way things were going I didn't want there to be any confusion about people's names. So I just turned Mr. Johansen toward you. I knew that Alfie had hired you, or was going to very shortly, so . . ."

"So you wanted me to blow the whistle."

"I wanted Judge Johansen to know where his son was, for the sake of both of them. There'd been a lot of heartbreak there. I hoped maybe the judge could straighten it out if he had a chance. He's a good man. I hoped Alfie would go home and forget about all this other stuff."

"Did he ever tell you that he was an undercover cop?"

"Alfie?" Lunceford laughed softly. "He's told me so many dumb damned things . . . maybe he did, I don't remember."

"An informer for the FBI?"

"I don't think so."

"Shortly before she died," I said, "Elaine Suzanne told me that she and Craig had been secretly married recently. Do you know anything about that?"

He gave me a dumb look. "Not unless . . ."

"Unless what?"

"Unless it was something to do with the plan. Maybe they did get married. I can see Elaine doing that, but Alfie . . well, for some devious purpose maybe, something to do with this crazy plot he was hatching."

"What do you think he was really going for, Johnny?"

Lunceford scratched his nose, looked at his hand, said very softly, "I think he was setting up some kind of blackmail. I believe he really got the idea in his head that he could take this show on the road. I think he was trying for Mafia money. What do you think?"

I told him, "If that is true, then I think he was crazy. Those people just don't play that kind of game."

Lunceford sighed as he replied, "That's what I figured. And that is why I didn't want any part of it."

I asked, "Where had Alfie been living since his apartment caught fire?"

He snickered, looked at the bandstand then back to me. "He's never had an apartment since he came here. He's just been living from house to house as long as someone would put up with him. He even stayed with Judith for awhile."

I raised an eyebrow at that. "She kicked him out?"

"Sure. It only took her about a week to figure him out. Then he moved in with Mack and Janie. You know they are really very nice people, the best. I don't know what kind of sob story he gave them but . . . well, they're just nice people. They took him in. The next day he put a move on Janie. She told Mack. Mack beat the shit out of him and tossed him out. He just kept moving on like that, house to house." Lunceford shook his head sorrowfully. "I think you're right. The guy was crazy. He was a user."

"Drugs?"

"No. People. And he could do it because he was so damned likeable. But, no, he couldn't bear to let people like him. Always had to screw it up with something dumb."

"Ever know him to use drugs?"

"Not recently. Back in college, you know, a joint now and then. Most everybody did that."

"Any of the other kids in the show have a drug habit?"

"Not that I know about. I mean, not unless someone was passing it around. Takes money, otherwise."

"Some people," I reminded him, "deal just enough to support a habit. You ever see anything to make you wonder about that?"

"No."

"There was a good supply of coke found in the apartment where Elaine and the three other guys were killed. Any idea where that could have come from?"

Lunceford said, "I didn't know those guys very well. Elaine, yeah, long time, we worked at the Curtain Call together and before that at La Mirada Civic Opera but . . . Elaine was very naive but she knew about drugs and what they do to a promising career. I can't believe she would mess around like that."

"But the guys . . ."

"I wouldn't call them seriously committed to anything," he replied quietly. "Except maybe to kinky sex."

"They were into that."

"Yeah. No holds barred. I warned Alfie about them but . . . turned out they were the only ones would put up with him. That's where he'd been staying the past few weeks."

"In that apartment?"

"That's right."

"Did Elaine know that?"

"Sure, she had to know. She lived right around the corner."

"In the apartment where Alfie was killed?"

"No, not that one. But in the same complex. Susan has lived there a long time. It's fairly convenient to the theater, so when someone needed an apartment she'd always steer them there. Nice place, nice area, low rent. What more can you want?"

I asked him, "Who lived in the apartment where Alfie was killed?"

"I really don't know," he replied. "Susan might know." I saw a thought cross his face. "Has anyone notified Judge Johansen?"

I said, "The sheriff probably notified him. They identified Alfie by his fingerprints."

"That wasn't necessary," he said. "I told them all about it."

"You did?"

"Yes, I told that detective, what's his name?—Lahey?"

"Lahey."

"Yeah, I told him. I just hope they notified the judge."

"He's really a judge?"

Lunceford chuckled grimly. "I guess he is. He's on the Minnesota Supreme Court."

"I see," I said.

But I hadn't seen anything yet.

CHAPTER 26

THE CONTENT OF the room had changed somewhat during the break, people coming and going, and when the band returned to the stage it appeared that most of the *La Mancha* cast were now present in the lounge and partying, though in a somewhat subdued manner.

"This is our usual night to howl," Lunceford told me. "Not Saturday because we do two shows on Sundays and it's already short enough between curtain-down on Saturday night and curtain-up on Sunday afternoon. It's going to be kind of strange around here tonight though."

He received another introduction from the stage, shook my hand and muttered something unintelligible, then went up amid howls and whistles from his friends to sing another song.

I looked at my watch and wondered what was keeping Judith, but then the cocktail waitress came over to my table and asked me, "Are you Joe Copp?"

"Guilty," I confessed.

"Judith asked me to tell you that she had to run an errand." She smiled. "But I don't think you're stood up." She handed me a slip of paper with a phone number scrawled across it. "Wants you to call her after one o'clock."

I took the paper and asked the waitress, "What time do you close?"

"Last call is one o'clock," she said.

"That's when the band signs off?"

"Well, not always on Fridays." She waved a hand to indicate the overflow crowd. "The cast from the theater comes in here to jam and entertain one another. A lot of the regulars stay for that too. So it's anybody's guess when the band goes home on Fridays. But remember, last call for drinks is one o'clock."

"How 'bout on Tuesday nights?"

"No, that's just on Fridays."

"Did you work this past Tuesday?"

"Uh huh, I work Tuesday through Saturday."

"The band too?"

"Uh huh." She was growing agitated. "Sorry, I've got drinks up."

"Just one more. Did anything unusual happen in here Tuesday night?"

She laughed and told me, "Something unusual happens in here every night."

"Do you remember seeing Craig Maan in here Tuesday night?"

It was like I had slapped her in the face. She stared at me in speechless reaction for a moment, then spluttered, "If that's your idea of a joke . . . !"

I held up both hands and said, "Hey, no, I didn't know I was on sensitive ground. I'm investigating his murder. I just wondered—"

"Well, lots of luck!" She swept the room with her arm. "Here are a few of your suspects, everyone in this room!

That jerk dirtied every person he touched! Hell, no, he wasn't here Tuesday because I promised him I'd poison his next drink in this bar!"

The waitress went away with that, and I could see that she was still steaming as she picked up a tray of drinks at the bar. I'd sure touched a nerve there.

The one man band was playing the intro to a show tune and Lunceford was sharing a microphone with the blonde, looking a little nervous and clowning with a table of kids down front while awaiting his musical cue. I left money on the table and went out of there, returned to the theater, found it locked and darkened.

An errand? At midnight?

There were things I needed to discuss with Judith White. That was the primary cause of disappointment, but I'll admit that also I'd been looking forward to just being with her again. I was no longer worried for her safety. If her own father was no longer worried, why should I be?

Well, okay, maybe I was worried just a bit. For sure I was feeling a growing agitation, or maybe apprehension, maybe something else.

Lunceford's characterization of Alfie Johansen, aka Craig Maan, had been a bit jumbled, even contradictory. Everyone had loved Alfie, Lunceford said, and yet it seemed that also everyone hated him once they got to know him. The waitress's reaction had been like an exclamation point to everything Lunceford told me. Apparently the guy had used people, lied to them, probably conned them. Judith had sort of indicated the same ambivalent feelings about the guy. Yet she hadn't bothered to tell me that she'd taken him home for a week. That was personal, of course, none of my business . . . but still I would have preferred that she instead of Lunceford had told me that.

She hadn't told me about Jimmy DiCenza either. Surely she had known that Jimmy was Vin's kid or she would have put something together about the name, especially since she'd told me that she'd kept up on the news about the trial in her father's courtroom.

Maybe she hadn't told me many things.

I decided I wanted to go up to her house. If she wasn't there, I'd wait for her. But then as I was walking toward my car, which was one of only a few remaining in that area, I spotted another car that looked familiar. Looked like the car that Art Lahey had been driving, so I detoured that way for a closer look.

It was Lahey's car, yeah.

Lahey was in it, sort of slumped down behind the steering wheel. There was congealed blood all around the lower half of his face, soaked into his coat and shirt, and a revolver lay across his lap. He'd been dead awhile.

I gingerly opened the door and leaned inside for a better view, saw that he'd been shot in the head or else in the mouth and the bullet had blown open the back of his skull as it tore through. Didn't see any sign of the bullet lodged in the roof and there was no broken glass, but I didn't do a thorough examination, instead went around to the other side and searched the glove box but found nothing of any importance in there.

So I carefully lifted the matted coat front and felt inside, found a sticky leather-covered notebook in the breast pocket. The revolver looked like the same one I'd left lying beside him earlier that day when he'd tried to arrest me—the one that he accused me of taking away—but a Police

Positive is a very common revolver and they all look pretty much alike.

I took the notebook and left everything else exactly as it lay, wiped everything I'd touched, and got the hell away from there.

I couldn't even report it, see, and I wished like hell that I hadn't been within twenty miles of the place when it went down.

But I had.

I'd spent the entire evening there.

And so, it appeared, had Lahey.

You'd think that someone would have heard a gunshot—hotel security cops, someone—in that still neighborhood toward the top of the evening. But sounds can be tricky and many people are not able to discriminate between the sound of a gun and other sounds that occur in the night . . . a single gunshot anyway, from within a closed car. It had to have happened while I was inside the theater, judging from the condition of the corpse, and certainly no one in there would have heard it over the amplified sounds within the theater. They don't use a live band but a recorded musical track, and it's pretty loud. Besides, you're just not focused on outside sounds when the show is in progress.

But someone had blown the man away probably within minutes after he'd walked away from me at the beginning of the third act.

Why?

He'd been disciplined and removed from the case, suspended from the force because of . . .

Because of what?

He'd said insubordination and threatening a superior, then he'd said, "How many do you want?"

I thought he'd meant how many more reasons for his suspension and I honestly had not thought to ask.

But why blow the man away? Obviously because he'd come too close to a truth that was making someone nervous. But what?

I didn't have a clue to that. I hoped, though, that I would find one in the bloodstained notebook—and I decided that I would not go to Judith's right away, after all.

I went back into the lounge, instead. Not to talk to anyone in particular but merely for personal comfort, to make myself as visible as possible until someone else discovered Lahey's body. If the gun that killed him was the same gun I'd taken away from him earlier, and if his report of the incident made it look as though I had kept the gun . . . well, I could be in deep shit again.

So I left my car where it stood and returned to the lounge, merely to look good.

I felt bad for Lahey, sure.

But I'll have to be honest. I felt even worse for myself. And I began to feel bad for Judith again, too. Hell, I felt bad for everyone.

The impossible dream had become a fullblown nightmare.

CHAPTER 27

I WAS IN a lousy mood when I went back into the lounge. My absence had not taken many ticks off the clock, probably no one had noticed it. My coffee and the money I'd laid down was still on the table and the place was still standing-room-only. Since no one had grabbed the table, the presumption must have been that I'd gone to the men's room or whatever. Lunceford was still on stage with *The Show Band* and they were concluding a rousing trio performance of a number from *Chorus Line*.

So much can occur between the ticks of a clock. Not in real time, especially, but in mental time. Lahey had been dead quite awhile. That murder had occurred in real time, my perception of it in mental time—and a lot had been happening inside my mind ever since. Guess I was reorganizing the case file, re-comparing the bits and pieces of data and looking at them in a different light, changing the focus of the police mind.

That sort of thing happens spontaneously, it is not a consciously directed activity but an eruption from the underbrain where all the bits and pieces had been stewing and bubbling and trying to fit themselves into a meaningful pattern. I have been told that the underbrain works that way, that it doesn't reason in a linear movement as the conscious brain reasons but that it gathers all the mental perceptions like in a big pot and organizes them cubicly into a three-dimensional continuum. Feed it enough data and it will inevitably come up with the true picture, because that is its function, that's the way it works, but then it's up to the linear mind to bring the picture forward into consciousness and that is where we usually get stupid, in that process of converting the cubic reality to a linear one—it's a process of interpretation and sometimes we get the effect ahead of the cause or else we lose one or the other entirely—but it's all still there in the underbrain and the pressure down there keeps increasing until we get it right in consciousness.

I don't know if that is true or not but I have seen evidence that the police mind seems to work that way, and I have seen my own mind take a sudden leap from stupidity to knowledge, just like that, in a flash, and then wonder why I had not seen the picture that way all the while.

Something like that was trying to happen as I sat in the lounge that night with my coffee and my thoughts, and I was aware that it was trying to happen—as though two of me were sitting there trying to communicate with each other but not quite getting through.

Then Susan Baker came in and sat down beside me, and the pressure suddenly became intense.

We just sat there for a minute or two, neither acknowledging the presence of the other. Lunceford came down off the stage and joined a group of cast members up front. The band struck up a number on their own and the blonde promised one and all that the party had only just begun.

I lit a cigarette, offered one to Susan, she declined. Guess that broke the ice.

She wrinkled her nose at the cigarette smoke and told me, "You should try to become drug-free."

I said, "Never looked at it that way, I guess. I think about cancer."

"You don't have to get cancer," she said soberly. There was still a touch of hoarseness in her voice. "But you should try to control your own body. Don't let it order you around like that."

I looked at the cigarette, thought about it, put it out. "You control yours, I guess," I said, looking at her admiringly. "Doing a pretty good job. Except with the throat."

She made a face at me, said, "I've been working on that."

The waitress came by, checked my cup and refilled it, looked at Susan. Susan ordered water, no ice. The waitress walked away with a sour face.

"Check yourself out of the hospital?"

She was working at her hair, trying to tie the cascading flow into a loose bun at the shoulders. "No reason not to," she replied. "I'm fine now. Besides, I couldn't afford it. Thanks for the money. I used it to bail myself out of there. No insurance."

I said, "You'd probably be better off there for awhile, insurance or no. This thing isn't settled yet, Susan."

"I know," she said lightly. She gave up on the hair, allowed it to go back into freefall. "I'm not afraid to die. Death is an illusion anyway. I just want to make sure—when it's my time, I don't want it to be like I haven't lived."

"Do you feel that you may be dying soon?"

"There's always that possibility, isn't there. Were you born with a guarantee?"

I chuckled, said, "No one ever showed it to me."

"You're nice," she told me. "I just wanted to say thanks. And I'm sorry I yelled at you today."

The waitress brought the water, moved quickly on without a word.

"How nice am I?"

She smiled. "Nice enough."

"Nice enough," I said, "to be in big trouble."

"You created that for yourself," she told me.

I said, "Like hell I did. Someone very cleverly created it for me. I think you know who. I think you know why. So if you really want to thank me . . ."

Such a beautiful girl. She sighed, did some stretches above her head, said something I didn't hear. The noise level in there was rather high.

"Didn't hear that," I told her.

She placed a small hand on my thigh, bent forward to look intently into my eyes and said to me, "Can we get out of here?"

"Not right away," I said.

"We can't talk in here with all this noise."

"We could try. I can't leave right now."

She showed me a pout, asked, "What do you want to know?"

"Did you know what was going down last night?"

"I don't know what you mean."

"Were you in that apartment next door to you?"

"I've been in there, sure. But not last night. Elaine was supposed to bring you to my place."

"For what?"

She shook her head. "I didn't understand that part of it.

I was just told that Elaine would bring you there and I was supposed to keep you there until . . ."

"Until what?"

"Until Craig sent for you, I guess."

"Was it planned that Craig would walk off just before the curtain?"

"I guess so, yes."

"Why?"

"Well . . . as I understood it . . . it all had to be done last night. The show is scheduled to close next week and time was of the essence."

"All what had to be done last night?"

"It all had to be settled. And Craig had to have some time to . . . do whatever he had to do, I guess."

"And your part?"

She gave me half a smile, a very seductive one. "All I had to do was keep you entertained."

"Until Craig sent for me."

"As I understood it, yes."

"But the plan backfired."

"I guess it did. Craig is dead, isn't he."

"What was I supposed to do? Where did I fit into the plan?"

She shrugged and replied, "You're a detective, aren't you. I guess you were supposed to do what detectives do."

I smiled grimly. "Jump out of a closet or something?"

"Maybe."

"The guys next door were all set up with a video camera. Who was supposed to be the victim? Not me."

"Oh no, not you," she assured me. "But I don't know who . . ."

"A blackmail scheme."

She said, "If you choose to look at it that way."

"What other way could you look at it?"

"Karma," she said with another half-smile.

"I thought karma is God's business," I replied.

"Well, who is God?" she asked teasingly.

"Not Craig, surely."

"In a way, sure. You're God. I'm God. We're all God."

I said, "Then God is kind of screwed up, isn't he."

She tossed her head and replied, "It just seems that way sometimes. Look, Joe, this is just an act. It's all an act."

"What do you mean?"

"This play was cast before we were even born. We tried out for the parts and won the roles and came down here to put them on the stage. You could remember that if you tried."

I tried, but I couldn't remember any of it. I told her so, and I asked her, "Do you remember what happens to me at the end?"

She said, "You're patronizing me. I don't like that."

I said, "No, I believe you are patronizing me."

"I'm not," she replied solemnly. "Look, we've all been together before, many times. That's the way it works, and we're trying to work out the karma that is between us. Why do you think we all got together this way?"

"It's the damned freeways," I told her. "Gridlock in the city. Speaking of that, who rents the apartment where Craig was killed?"

She showed me a blank face. "Where was he killed?"

I whipped out my notes, flipped through them in the dim light of the lounge, told her, "Your complex, number 3H. Who lives there?"

"That must be . . ."

"Who?"

"You'd better ask Judith White."

"Why should I do that?"

"Judith lived in the same complex once upon a time. I guess before she moved back in with her dad. She's the one who sent me there. The owners don't stand on formality the way some places do. You just pay your rent and move in, there's no first and last, no deposits, and nobody bothers you. It's ideal for people in our business."

"What do you think of Judith?"

"She's okay, I guess. A bit prim. Nothing wrong with her a little poverty wouldn't cure. Judith doesn't know what it's like down in the trenches. Born rich and that makes a bitch—and that's no pitch." Susan laughed, and it had a touch of bitterness. "But it's her karma."

"How rich?" I wanted to know.

"Old money on her mother's side. Judith inherited quite a lot. She owns that house."

"What house?"

"The house she kicked her dad out of."

I didn't know how to respond to that. While I was thinking about it, Susan added, "And of course she owns the theater."

"What theater?" I asked stupidly.

"The dinner theater. Not the building, that's hotel property, but she leases it. She owns the damned theater."

Well, I didn't know how to respond to that either. And Susan was apparently getting bored with me. She said, "Look, you stay as long as you like but I've got to get out of here. Can't stand this smoke in here. This is your last chance. I'm leaving."

I sighed and said, "Goodnight, Susan."

But I felt more like saying "good grief" and, yeah, I felt a bit like Charlie Brown—I just couldn't seem to get this one right.

One by one and two by two the cast of *La Mancha* got up and did their numbers with the band while I sat in a near stupor from the tug of war inside my brain. Trying to make sense of it, dammit. Trying to make sense of . . .

Too many issues that may or may not be related were clouding the picture, I was sure of that. What did I have? I had the Mafia, for Christ's sake, I had United States Marshals and the FBI, I had a nationally sensitive trial and the Witness Protection Program, nervous politicians and compromised cops—a *dead* cop now—a rich judge's rich daughter and Jimmy DiCenza and the Minnesota Supreme Court—good grief, Charlie Brown, I had a pot running over, and buried in all that I had a bunch of talented kids with impossible dreams and maybe a bit too much reach for the grasp.

I took a leaf from Susan's book and decided to control my own body, *ordered* the brain to get off its ass and do its work, and I even tried to remember things I'd never known that I knew.

But none of it was working, not in full light, and I knew that I had to do better than that before the sheriffs came knocking at my door again.

I knew, too, that the sheriffs could be coming fearsome quick now. From somewhere outside my dark gloom I heard sirens clattering about the premises and everybody in the room heard them too. The band took another "short break" and went down to converse soberly with their friends in the audience. The bartender closed the bar and shortly thereafter a waiter came in from one of the banquet rooms at the far side of the building to announce to the hushed room, "There are cops all over out there. They've found another murder. Some guy got shot in his car."

Several patrons got up and left immediately but the gang from *La Mancha* seemed to be huddling even closer now. I fingered the bloodstained notebook inside my coat pocket and wondered if I should try to stash it somewhere, went to the men's room and concealed it behind a towel rack, got back to my table just a few steps ahead of the sheriffs.

We were in for a long one, I knew that. They went from table to table, taking down names and checking IDs, asking the same questions table by table. I showed them my driver license and told them I'd been on the premises all evening, hadn't heard or seen anything unusual or suspicious. Thought I'd gotten away with it until a sergeant came over a few minutes later and asked me, "Aren't you Joe Copp, the private investigator?"

I admitted it.

He told me, "Captain Waring would like some words with you."

I asked, "Where is he?"

"At the murder scene. Come on. Let's go."

Well, so what the hell, I was moving up in the world. You don't usually get a captain responding to a homicide. This, of course, was not your ordinary homicide—this was one of their own, suspended or not.

Waring was familiar, I'd seen the face before, very smooth guy with a military haircut dressed out like a Wall Street banker. He was standing beside Lahey's car with one arm on the roof and a very sad face. He gave me a contemptuous look and asked me, "That your car over there?"

He pointed to it and I replied, "That's mine, yeah."

"How long has it been there?"

I looked at my watch, did a fast calculation, told him, "Long enough for the engine to go cold. Check it out."

"Already did. You've been around all evening?"

"Since just before intermission for *La Mancha*, yeah." I peered inside the car. "That Lahey in there?"

"What's left of him," the captain replied. He looked even sadder and asked, "Why do cops always put the barrel of the gun in their mouths? Why is that?"

I shrugged, told him, "It's hard to miss, that way."

"Guess it is," he said.

"That the way you're reading it? He did himself?"

"Seems obvious, doesn't it," Waring said. "The sergeant had a bad day. It's his own gun. Why do you suppose he came here to do it?"

I said, "He came here to talk to me." I told the captain about it, then added, "I don't think he did himself. He wasn't despondent. Mad as hell but not despondent. He was still working the case."

"What case?"

"The multiple murder case from last night, the one he was suspended from—or weren't you involved in that?"

"Don't get smart with me, Joe," the captain said but not in an angry way. But his interest in me seemed to have quickened a bit. "What are you doing here?"

"I'm on a case," I told him.

"Who's the client?"

I jerked my head toward the theater. "Them," I said. "All

of them, the kids in the cast. They took up a collection and hired me to find out what's happening to them."

"What *is* happening to them?"

"Don't have that figured out yet," I replied. "That's why I'm here tonight."

"That case has been closed."

"What case has been closed?"

"The murder case you were talking about. The case that Lahey couldn't let go of. It's closed. It's best you go on home now and just let it stay that way."

I showed him a sympathetic smile and said, "Yeah, but I've got these clients, see, and they don't want it closed."

"You want a court order?"

"I'd take one of those, sure. And, uh, include Lahey's murder in there, why don't you."

The guy spun on his heel and walked away. Nobody else seemed interested in me, so I went away too, got in my car and drove off clean.

Why?

Why did they let me off clean?

I threw that into the pot and pointed the car toward San Antonio Heights.

Maybe Judith could start my pot to boiling, I thought. Or cool it down forevermore.

CHAPTER 28

SHE HAD COMPANY—a big Mercedes in the driveway and lots of lights showing inside the house.

Judith answered the doorbell, and I thought for a moment she wasn't going to let me in. "You were supposed to call," she said, sounding a bit embarrassed.

"Tried that," I told her. "Didn't work."

"When?"

"At one o'clock."

"I told you *after* one, Joe."

I looked at my watch. "That's what it is now. So am I coming in?"

She said, "I'm not alone."

"I can see that," I told her. "Still want to come in."

"Just a minute," she said and closed the door but not all the way. I heard her speaking to someone inside, then she threw the door wide and invited me in with a noticeable lack of enthusiasm.

I recognized him instantly from the portraits I'd seen earlier, a suavely handsome man of obvious culture, rather slightly built but a leonine head with every hair in place and looking good—youthful appearance, an almost gentle face, soft eyes, about a head shorter than me—not exactly what you would envision as a "hanging judge" but a guy I would like to see on the bench if my life were at stake.

"Sorry if I'm intruding, Your Honor," I said without any introduction. "Things are happening fast and I really need to talk with your daughter. And with you too," I added, "if that's okay."

He waved off both the apology and the explanation, told me, "I was just leaving, Mr. Copp."

"Stay awhile," I suggested. "You could find it very interesting."

He exchanged glances with Judith, smiled at me, returned to his chair.

I told Judith, "Art Lahey is dead."

She seemed to be shocked by that news, maybe a little dazed."You mean the police sergeant?"

"That's the one I mean, yeah." I told the judge, "He reacted negatively to the habeas corpus for your two marshals, had a fight with his superiors, got suspended. A few hours later he got dead. I wonder why, Your Honor."

The judge looked at me with a level stare and replied, "That's unfortunate. Of course, it's impossible to predict every implication of every decision one makes but . . . I'm truly sorry to hear it. How did it happen?"

I said, "His captain thinks he sucked up a gun barrel and pulled the trigger on himself. I don't think so. I had a long talk with Lahey minutes before he died and he did not sound like a despondent or depressed or desperate man to me. I believe he was murdered."

"That is the risk every police officer assumes," the judge said in a somewhat sympathetic voice. "Brave men. They live in constant jeopardy. It's too bad."

"I believe," I said, "that it has something to do with the DiCenza case."

The judge held up a hand and said, "Please, Mr. Copp, you must understand that I cannot and will not discuss that case with anyone, nor do I want to hear any reference or any allusion to the defendant in the case."

"Not even," I said, "with your daughter's life hanging in the balance? I respect your protocols, sir, but you must know that you cannot isolate yourself within a bubble and let the whole world go crash for the sake of your protocols."

He got to his feet and turned to his daughter, kissed her coolly on the cheek, and flat walked out the door. I couldn't believe it.

I looked at Judith and said, "Well maybe he can."

"He always could," she replied quietly.

And that was all we had to say about the judge, for the moment. She flung herself into my arms and we didn't have a lot to say about anything for quite a long while. I even forgot about Lahey, and DiCenza, and all the dead kids. I forgot about everything—and that, I guess, illustrates the power of eros. Earlier I called it anesthesia. Sometimes, maybe, it is more like sanctuary. Whatever it is, apparently we both needed it desperately.

It was three o'clock and we were sprawled across the big bed in Judith's upstairs bedroom, totally spent in that sweet exhaustion that comes only in the wake of a perfect and prolonged mingling of sexual energies. She was lying atop me with both arms curled about my neck, golden head on my shoulder and soft lips at my ear, and she was quietly weeping.

I told her, "Makes me nervous when the lady cries

afterward, never know if it's tears of joy, guilt or disappointment."

She kneed me gently in the groin and replied, "It's sure not disappointment, dummy. Did you ever consider sheer exhaustion as a cause?"

"That bad, eh?"

"That good," she corrected me, snuggling closer for direct emphasis. And after a moment, "Joe . . . ?"

"Yes ma'am?"

"Life is too complicated."

"Agreed."

"Let's run away. Tahiti. Somewhere very basic."

"I hear New Zealand is nice."

"Let's go to New Zealand then."

"Don't think my Visa could stand it. How 'bout Catalina or San Diego?"

"I'm serious," she said with a pout.

"So'm I."

That seemed to have ended that line of conversation. After a brief silence, she withdrew to a position with her forearms supporting her weight on my chest, looked at me very soberly and said, "I can't figure out my dad."

"Have you really tried?"

"Yes. For years. I believe the man is totally devoid of passion."

I slapped her lightly on the bottom and told her, "Well I guess you take after your mother."

"I didn't mean that kind of passion," she said, still very serious. "I mean, he never has any emotions. Never laughs, never cries, never gets angry, never gets glad. He's just . . ."

"A judge," I suggested.

"A cold fish," she decided.

"That's no way to talk about your dad," I told her. "I had the impression that you two had a very good relationship. Don't uh, judge him too harshly in this present matter. He's doing what he has to do."

She said, "It isn't that. It's everything else. He was the same way with my mother. She died of cancer, and it wasn't a terribly prolonged death, she died six weeks after the diagnosis. I never saw him cry, Joe. Never saw him look saddened, or frightened, or even regretful. He just remained aloof from the whole thing, never once made himself vulnerable to it."

"You didn't see him in his private moments," I reminded her. "Some men go to the closet to weep."

She shook her head. "Not my dad."

She got up then and went into the bathroom, leaving me with thoughts of the judge in the case. After a moment I heard water running in the shower, and I knew that another idyll had ended.

Over breakfast I casually asked Judith, "Why didn't you tell me that you own the theater?"

She replied, just as casually, "I don't remember you asking about it."

I said, "Not in so many words, maybe."

"Do you go around telling people that you own the Joe Copp Detective Agency? Anyway, I don't own the theater. I have the production contract."

"Do you have a boss?"

"No."

"Then you own it. Also, you didn't tell me that you brought Craig Maan home with you for a week."

"What is this?" she asked teasingly. "Kiss and tell time? You want to give me a list of all the women you've taken home with you? But it wasn't like that with Craig. I let him use the maid's quarters until he could find a place." She showed me a wicked look. "Of course, I won't say that it could not have been like that with Craig, at first, if he'd shown any inclination."

"But he didn't."

"No. Who've you been talking to?"

"Everyone I could find," I admitted. "I heard you kicked him out. Why?"

"Well, not because he wouldn't play house with me. He just took too many liberties around here."

"What kind of liberties?"

"Snooping, stealing, those kind of liberties."

"Tell me about it."

"No big deal," she said, trying to dismiss the whole thing.

"No, it could be important," I persisted.

"He stole money from me. Okay?"

"Not okay. Why didn't you fire him?"

"He didn't steal from the theater. He stole from me. I try to keep the perspectives separated."

"You said he was snooping. Tell me about that."

She said, "Joe . . ."

I said, "Tell me."

"He was too interested in my dad. Okay?"

"Not okay. Why shouldn't he be interested in your dad? I'm interested in your dad."

"It wasn't like that. He actually rummaged through my things, dug out old photo albums, kept bugging me to introduce him to Daddy. Hey, I didn't need that. And I don't need this, Joe."

I told her, "Come on, snap out of that, this could be important. The guy was a con artist. He was trying to set something up when he got himself killed. I need to know what was going on."

"Why don't you just let it go?" she cried.

"Let it go? Let it *go?* Come on, Judy, you can't let something like this go! Five people are dead, six now, and the sixth was a cop investigating the other five deaths! I can't let this go!"

"Well why not? Leave well enough alone! You're just going to dig up all kinds of trash, that's all! Let's just go away and forget about it!"

"You're serious about going away?"

"Yes I am."

"What about your theater?"

"I know people who would love to take it over for me for awhile."

"I am not a rich man, Judy."

"That's okay. I'm a rich woman."

"So I've been told. How rich?"

"Rich enough."

"Is your dad rich?"

She blinked at that. "You're still digging."

"Is he?"

She blinked again. "No, but he does okay."

"Why isn't he rich?"

"Because he had a premarital agreement drawn up before he married my mother. Didn't want to be tainted by her money. Damn him!"

"Why damn him, Judith?"

"She gave him everything, her career, her fortune, her adoration, she gave him everything."

"And what did he give her in return?"

"He gave her the judge," she said quietly.

"I see," I said.

"And he gave her cancer."

"It's not contagious, kid."

"Oh yes it is. The emptiness is. You have to fill emptiness with something. My mother filled it with cancer."

"You inherited her money?"

"Yes."

"And her emptiness?"

"I guess so."

"Are we going for the cancer now?"

She looked at me, almost cried, said, "Dammit, Joe."

"Did Craig ever meet your dad?"

"Go to hell, will you."

I said, "Maybe you took after your dad, after all."

She said, "Okay, he met him."

"When?"

"Way back at the beginning. The day I ran him off."

"Tell me about it."

"There's nothing to tell. Dad and I had a dinner date. He was in the midst of the DiCenza trial but dinner together twice a month in this family is religion. The show was still a bit wobbly. Craig had played Cervantes in college but he really did not know the role that well and he was struggling with it, so I was struggling too. I was working with Craig, trying to—well, anyway, I took time away and had dinner with Dad. At the hotel. I'd left Craig at the theater. He crashed our dinner."

"Just like that."

"Yes. Did the whole act, you know—surprise, surprise, didn't know you were eating here, that sort of thing. Of course I had to introduce him to my dad."

"And?"

"And nothing. They sat and talked law. I was surprised that Craig knew so much about it. He said that he used to enjoy long after-dinner conversations with Judge Johansen, Johnny's dad."

"How'd they get along?—Craig and your dad?"

"They got along fine. But I was fuming."

"Why?"

"Maybe because I hate to be crashed in on. Maybe because I already knew that Craig was a rat and I was suspicious."

"Suspicious of what?"

"I don't know. I had already become uneasy about Craig's interest in dad. And I had already refused several times to introduce them."

"What were you afraid of?"

"I wasn't afraid of anything. Just hate to be used."

"You weren't afraid that Craig might say something to your dad that would embarrass you?"

"Well . . . I don't know. Maybe so."

"Did Craig know Jimmy DiCenza?"

She gave me a long, searching look before responding to that. "So you have been talking to a lot of people."

"You knew that Vincent DiCenza was Jimmy's old man."

"Of course I knew." A tear popped out of one eye and slid down her nose. She dabbed at it with her napkin, said, "Joe . . . you'd better stop there."

"Can't stop there, kid," I replied as gently as I could. "The truth will out. Let's do it now, before someone beats us to it."

She said, "It's not very pretty."

"Life often isn't. That doesn't mean we have to hide it. Usually it's best to just confront it. Save a lot of anxieties that way, and usually the anxieties are worse than anything else. Tell me about you and Jimmy."

"I was in one of his shows," she said quietly. "Long time ago. A lifetime ago."

"You're not that old."

"You get old quick in this business. One day can equal an ordinary lifetime. I didn't want to be ordinary. And I'd promised my mom that I'd pick up where she left off." Judith dabbed at her eyes again. "I tried. Just couldn't take it anymore. Jimmy was . . ."

"What?"

"Exciting, I guess. And I hadn't gotten old yet. He booked me on the Japanese circuit. Found out very quick that I was not over there just to dance."

"So what'd you do?"

"I danced. With Japanese businessmen. And afterward I danced in their beds."

"Why?"

She raised a hand and dropped it in a "what the hell" gesture. "Seemed the only thing to do. I told you to leave it alone, Joe."

"Told you I couldn't. Neither can you. That was then. This is now. It wasn't for the money. You didn't need that. So why?"

"Would you be shocked if I told you that I rather enjoyed it?"

"Not necessarily."

"Well, sometimes I did. The Japanese can be very charming with Western women, very gallant, entirely flattering. And these were not shopkeepers. They were the movers and shakers in that country."

"Politicians too?"

"Possibly. I never asked."

"You and Jimmy still on good terms?"

"No reason not to be. He was always a gentleman with me. I never tied him in with anything actually criminal, and I'd never heard of Vincent DiCenza until he entered my dad's courtroom."

"Jimmy tells me that you send him girls."

"Jimmy is mistaken. I refer talent to him when it seems appropriate."

"For his Japanese circuit."

"Or whatever. He packages and books, and a kid can actually make a good living with Jimmy."

"And grow old quickly," I suggested.

She sighed. "That too. But I don't try to make those decisions for people."

"People," I suggested, "like Susan Baker and Elaine Suzanne."

"I am more discriminating than that," she said.

"Jimmy isn't. I've seen his indiscriminations."

"I am. I wouldn't refer flakes like those two. Are you enjoying this, Joe?"

"Not a lot," I said.

"Are you finished, then?"

"Not quite. You still owe me one. Did Craig know Jimmy DiCenza?"

She stared at me for a long time, then said, "We should have gone away, Joe."

Yeah. Yeah. We should have. She brushed my cheek with her lips as she said goodbye, then she went back upstairs and left me at the kitchen table with nothing but my thoughts and tumbling emotions.

It was four o'clock on Saturday morning, and I had to

go invade another day in a darkness more abysmal than ever, without even an illusion to light the way.

Big bad Joe, Copp For Hire, married to his job and to hell with everything else. And every *one* else, it seemed.

I was not that different, I decided, from the judge.

CHAPTER 29

IT'S NOT THAT far down into Ontario and it's a quick trip that time of morning. I made it in less than ten minutes and found the address from my copy of the cast file without difficulty—a small streetside apartment building near downtown, old but decent. The number I wanted was on the third flight up and Johnny Lunceford responded fairly quickly to the insistent pressure on the doorbell button.

He cracked the door with two safety chains still in place, reacted dumbly to my presence there, then sleepily told me, "Shit, man, I've got a pregnant wife. What are you doing here this time of night?"

"Justice never sleeps, Johnny," I replied. "Do I kick the door down, come in there and talk in your pregnant wife's face, or would you rather do it out here?"

No decision to it. He said, "Just a minute," and closed the door. Guess he went in to say something to his wife, he was gone less than a minute then joined me in the hallway wrapped in a bulky robe. "Jesus! What do you want?"

"I want it straight this time," I told him. "Off the top.

Alfie didn't come to you for sanctuary and you didn't get him the *La Mancha* role. So let's start again from there."

The guy had a desperate, trapped look about him, a frightened look, but that quickly gave way to bravado, defiance. "You're not a real cop! Where do you get off coming in here talking to me like that? Scare the shit out of my wife, she's going to have a baby, where do you get off?"

I showed him where, hoisted him two feet off the floor, let him drop. His knees buckled and he would have fallen onto his face if I hadn't been there to catch him and put him back on his feet—but not entirely on his feet. "I didn't want to get mean with you, Johnny," I told him. "I think you're a nice kid caught up in a hellish nightmare, but I can't let that get in my way now. Either we talk like friends or we talk mean, and I leave that up to you."

Again, no decision required. "Okay okay," he said quickly. "Let's talk friendly."

I told him, "I already gave you your cue, kid."

"We were in college together. That's true. I left two years ahead of him, that's true, had no further contact with him. Never really liked him. So it bombed me out of my skull when he turned up at East Foothills. Sort of bombed him too. He took me aside and said, 'Please don't tell anyone my real name. I'm on a case and I'm under cover.' I said okay. That's how it started."

"What kind of case?"

"He wouldn't say. I guessed narcotics. Then later we put together the story I told you."

"How much later?"

"Couple of weeks, I guess."

"He was already next to Judith White?"

"Sure. She brought him in to replace Greg Houston."

"*She* brought him in?"

"That's the way I saw it."

"And he was staying with her at the time?"

"I think so, yes."

'You ever hear of a guy called Jimmy DiCenza?"

"I don't think so. Oh! That's the guy that's on trial. Judith's father is hearing that case."

I said, "No, Jimmy is the son. He's a producer, sort of—packager and promoter. You never heard of Jimmy?"

"Uh . . . I don't think so. Well, maybe . . . I don't know. Last year when I was doing *South Pacific* with Judith, there was this guy . . . sort of hanging around on and off. Italian. I think he was a producer."

"But you never heard Alfie mention that name."

"No."

"Tell me about Elaine Suzanne."

"Her real name is Elaine Somoza. Very strange girl. Talented but strange. Had a thing for Alfie." He laughed quietly. "All the women get a thing for Alfie. He never knows they're alive."

I told him, "Just before she was killed, Elaine told me that she and Craig had been secretly married."

"You said that before but I don't know. Sounds like disinformation. Alfie was good at that. Tell enough lies, no one will ever know the truth."

"Yeah, tell me about it," I replied. "Why would someone want Elaine dead?"

"Same reason, I guess, they wanted Alfie dead."

"And what would that be?"

"Well . . ." Lunceford scratched his nose and thought about it, then replied, "Maybe he was telling the truth about being undercover."

"And all the other crap?—the lies?"

"Disinformation," he said with a sigh.

"You honestly don't know what he was trying to pull together the other night?"

"I honestly don't. I stayed away from it. Hell, I couldn't—I've got a kid on the way."

"Did you get to know Larry Dobbs and Jack Harney?"

"Not much. I stayed away from that too. Alfie first told me they were chasing him, then he told me they were his bodyguards—shit, then he came up with this crap that they were going to back a national road company."

"You didn't buy that?"

He gave a little shrug and said, "It would've been nice."

"Would you have gone on the road with them?"

"Sure. Chance like that comes all too seldom. But I guess I never really bought the whole ticket."

"Answer me this. Did you feel that Alfie, at any time, *really* thought that he was going to put this show on the road?"

Lunceford frowned and did a little stage posture with one foot in front of the other and a hand on the hip. Then he reversed the whole posture and gave me a frustrated look. "That guy," he said disgustedly, "was never committed to anything like this. He goofed off in college and I guess he goofed off after he left college. He had absolutely no professional experience as an actor. So why did Judith bring him in here?"

I said, "I guess I better find out why."

I thanked the impossible dreamer and sent him back to bed with his pregnant wife.

Then I resumed my own quest for the truth, the whole truth, and nothing but the truth.

But that impossible goal was still a long way off.

CHAPTER 30

I WENT BACK by the hotel and retrieved Lahey's notebook, then took it over to the allnight coffee shop and searched it for information. Lahey had been a good cop and he'd conducted a textbook investigation. One of the last things he'd told me was that he was following a lead—and the only clue I had to that was the blood-stained notebook that I'd lifted from his dead body.

It was rather cryptic, as these things usually are, jottings in a personal shorthand which no stenographer could decipher—but maybe another cop could—and I saw something in there that sent me back to the apartment complex where all the killings had gone down, all but Lahey's, and he was dead only because the others were dead.

I got the manager out of bed and looked at her records. The apartment in which Craig/Alfie was killed had been rented barely two months earlier by a Mary Todd Bernson, first month's rent paid in cash and the next by a postal money order received in the mail. The manager could not remember Mary Todd Bernson and she could not recognize any of the pictures from my cast file.

So I roused the neighbors on both sides and showed

them the pictures. Lady on the east side picked out Craig Maan, told me: "This one, I think, I've seen a couple of times, maybe three or four times, always at night. I thought that he was probably her son."

"Who's son?"

"The son of the lady who lived there. Didn't see much of her either, but I would say she was older, an older person, older than this young man."

"Did you ever talk to her?"

"No. I don't believe she was home much."

I had an idea, asked her: "Did you ever see her alone or was the son always here when she was here?"

She reflected on that, then told me, "You know, I just don't know. Come to think of it, I guess when I saw one I always saw the other very soon afterward."

"Did you ever see them together at the same time?"

Another reflection, then: "I don't think I ever did. But now I remember . . . a young woman was here once too. Oh, I would say, maybe last week sometime. Very pretty."

"You saw her go into the apartment?"

"No, I saw her coming out one night."

I thanked the lady and went on my way. Didn't know what I had, exactly, but knew that I had something I didn't have before.

That apartment 3H had not had a real tenant those past two months. It was a place for people to meet in secret, a blind. But I still did not know yet how to factor that information into what I thought I knew about this case. I simply had to keep on struggling, and I knew where to go next.

At five o'clock on a weekday morning you could expect to spend maybe a couple of hours of freeway time between my neck of the woods and Studio City, so I was glad it was Saturday; I made it in about forty minutes and reached the top of Coldwater Canyon at just past five-thirty. Wasn't quite daylight yet and the traffic in that area was almost non-existent.

Jimmy's cliffside joint lay brooding in the pre-dawn silence with only two small nightlights to break the darkness. I rolled to a stop in the half-moon drive with my engine off, quietly left the car and pulled the riot gun out of the trunk, scaled a wall and on up onto the roof of the house—over the top, so to speak, because the other side of that wall was a void everywhere except the area in which the house hung on steel beams projecting from the side of the cliff.

Didn't really know what kind of security Jimmy enjoyed and didn't particularly give a damn. I did know that the big double doors up front were three inches thick and featured kickbolts anchoring them to the cement floor—I'd checked that out when I was there earlier—so I was going for a softer point of entry. I remembered also that his fancy playboy bedroom that was probably copied from the Playboy Mansion itself featured a curving glass wall at the back of the house with sliding doors opening onto the garden patio.

I wanted to jar the guy awake and go for a bit of startled honesty, if honesty was possible with this guy—didn't want to give him any recovery-makeup moments—so I swung down off the flat rear roof onto the patio and immediately let go three quick rounds from the riot gun into the ceiling of his bedroom.

There were yards of glass and draperies in between, of course, but the draperies parted without any argument and the glass came raining down with a jangling roar, followed instantly by the whooping siren of a burglar alarm. An excited female voice inside immediately yelped, "Earthquake!" as I moved through the wreckage of the window. A bedside lamp flashed on to reveal three rudely awakened individuals galvanized by fear and struggling to get off the bed—Jimmy, sure, typically sandwiched between two naked sexpots—but tangled in the bedcovers as well as one another and having a rather undignified time with it.

Then Jimmy saw me and knew it was not an earthquake, but it may as well have been for his peace of mind. He spluttered, "What?—what . . . ?" and rolled his eyes up and tried to take cover behind one of the women.

I tossed the riot gun onto the patio then grabbed Jimmy and tossed him out behind it. He bounced hard off the decking and rolled across several feet of broken glass, instantly began bleeding from numerous small cuts and looked up at me with doomsday eyes as I caught up with him. He cried, "Joe! What the hell, Joe?"

"That's where you're headed, pal," I told him as I picked him up again and heaved him into the pool, then I grabbed a long-handled cleaning net and met him with it as he surfaced, following from the side of the pool and poking him with the metal handle to keep him treading water at the deep end until he was in total panic and utterly exhausted. Didn't take long; Jimmy hadn't kept himself in very good shape.

Meanwhile the alarm was still whooping and I guess the girls had snatched some clothing up and run away. Just as Jimmy was about to go down for the final count I heard a car gun away out front and saw the headlights flash against the cliff as it spun onto the roadway. I dropped the cleaning tool into the pool and told Jimmy, "Okay, hit the steps," and I met him there.

Poor guy was totally out of breath, shaking in terror or exhaustion or maybe both and still bleeding all over but I felt that I had to go for the big score and it had to be quick, so I picked him up by both ankles, went to the rail and hung him out to dry—several hundred feet above the canyon floor.

Maybe that was unnecessary because there was no fight in this guy. He gasped, "Jesus, Joe, don't do this. I'm all wet, you're gonna lose me."

I said, "We'll see how long I can hang on. How quick is your memory? I'm giving you two names. You decide which one you like best then talk to me about it—Alfred Johansen and Craig Maan—which do you like, Jimmy?"

Guy had a great memory, quick one too. "Craig was sent by Dom Pergano." Pergano was one of the family's legal eagles. "Vin wanted him stashed for awhile."

"Stashed where? For what?"

"That's what I wondered," Jimmy panted. "Kid had been doing gay shows back east somewhere. I got no gay shows."

"What kind of gay shows?"

"Uh, female impersonators, I guess."

"So why'd you send him to Judith?"

"Dom suggested it. Said the kid had done some musical theater. Uh, blood's going to my head, Joe. Gettin' dizzy."

"You were born dizzy," I told him. "Dom knew all about Judith, then."

"I guess I'd mentioned her. He said I should put Craig with Judith until Vin needed him."

"Until Vin needed him?"

"That's right."

"Needed him for what?"

"Jesus, I'm blacking out! I'm going to faint!"

"For *what?*" I insisted.

"I don't know for what!" Jimmy screamed. "Come on, Joe! Come on!"

"So why'd they hit 'im?"

"Did they? Jesus! I didn't know! I swear!"

I dropped one leg and the poor guy damn near had a heart attack on me but it was no time for pity. "Why'd they hit 'im, Jimmy?"

"He was FBI!" I was told by a totally terrified man.

"Come on. He wasn't old enough."

"Old enough to tell tales," Jimmy whispered.

The burglar alarm was still doing its thing and I have to admit that I'd lost all taste for this exercise. I swung the little mobster back onto his patio and dropped him there. He grunted, "Jesus, I'm bleeding all over."

"Be glad," I told him and left him there, retrieved my riot gun and went out through the house, got into my car and quickly put the scene behind me. I heard a distant police siren and saw the flashing lights winding up from Studio City so I went the other way, over the top and into Beverly Hills.

And since I was so close, anyway, I jogged on over to the Wilshire highrise district of West L.A. for a call on the judge in the case.

Female impersonator?—FBI informer?

I was beginning to see a light at the end of the tunnel, but didn't know if I wanted to come into that or not. But there was only one damned way left to go. So on I went.

I showed the doorman a hundred dollar bill and the cast pictures, asked him, "Ever see any of these come in here?"

He picked the man of La Mancha and said, "This one,

I guess, but it was quite awhile ago. Used to come in a lot."

"Do you know Judge White when you see him?"

"Yes, sir. Did you know there's blood all over your suit, sir?"

I showed him my badge and told him, "I got it honestly. Did you ever see Judge White with this man?"

"Not that I recall. I work midnight to eight. I usually see the judge in the mornings when he's leaving for work. But I saw him tonight. He came in—oh, I guess it must have been around three o'clock."

I tapped the photo. "When did you usually see this guy?"

"Usually in the middle of the night, sir. But not tonight. I haven't seen him since . . ."

"Coming and going?"

"That's right. But that's been, uh, probably a couple of months ago. I haven't seen him lately."

I surrendered the hundred bucks and went on up, hit the judge's doorbell several times but got no response, picked the lock and let myself in.

The entire apartment seemed to be in darkness except for a small lamp in the foyer casting muted light halfway into the living room. Judith sat in there in the semi-darkness, slumped onto a large leather recliner and obviously in a very down mood.

"What are you doing here?" she asked unemotionally.

"Looking for the light," I told her. "Go tell him I'm here."

"The judge is not in," she said in a muffled voice.

"Doorman says he is."

"Well, he went out again."

"So what are you doing, Judith?"

"Just thinking."

"Should've started that a long time ago," I said. "I just came from a heart to heart talk with Jimmy DiCenza. He told me some wild things. I wish you'd been the one who told me, kid."

"Told you what?"

"You never wondered why he sent Craig to you?"

She made an empty gesture with her hand as she replied, "Life is too complicated, Joe. We never know who to believe or what to believe, never know what's right and what's not. I stopped wondering long ago. And I'm not ashamed of anything I've ever done. What's *your* problem?"

I told her, "I'm not here to shame you. But I'd sure like to hear your version of the truth."

She showed me a sad little smile and asked, "The truth about what?"

"Who is Mary Todd Bernson?"

"Where'd you get that?"

"I picked it up. Who is she?"

A tear popped out of her eye and she replied, "Mary Todd Bernson was my mother."

"Maiden name."

"Yes."

"Did you know that Craig came to you by way of Vincent DiCenza?"

She sighed. "I've considered the possibility. Especially since . . . all this craziness began."

"Did he steal money from you?"

"No."

"What did Craig steal from you?"

"I guess he stole my dad," she whispered.

"You've known about your dad?"

"Wondered," she said quietly. "But I never knew for sure until . . . you should see his closet."

"I have, but what about it?"

"Did you see all the women's clothing?"

"Yes. Figured he had a live-in girlfriend."

She said, "So did I, until I looked closer. How odd. All the clothing in that closet was made for the same person."

I said, "That's uh . . ."

"He cheated me, Joe! He cheated my mother! Oh God, how could he . . . ?"

"Don't leap to conclusions, Judy."

". . . my own father, the great and wonderful and super respectable judge of all that's holy and noble . . ."

"Look, uh, you told me that you theater people take pride in your liberal attitude toward—"

"This isn't the theater, this is real, this is where people live. I never knew this man, Joe. Never knew him. Neither did Mother. We were married to a drag queen!"

"Maybe not," I told her, bleeding for her and wanting to protect her but knowing I couldn't. "Look at it from his point of view, try to understand what he tried to turn away from and give up for your sake, for her sake. Your mother has been dead a long time, Judy. Think of what the man has been living with."

"That's all I can think of," Judith replied bitterly. She got to her feet, gave me a sidewise look, asked me, "Can I go now?"

I said, "Dammit, kid, let's get square with each other."

"Too late for that," she told me. "None of it matters anymore anyway."

"Matters to me," I said.

"Not to me." She stepped past me and went on out.

I stood there for a moment trying to get myself together, lit a cigarette, wandered on through the living room and into the study, following a light source that turned out to be a small hi-intensity lamp on the judge's desk. He was there, too, but not as the judge. He wore a flowing pink negligee over other flimsy feminine things, slumped in his chair and staring emptily at a sheet of paper in the portable typewriter.

The judge was not in, right.

The judge was dead.

He'd sucked up the barrel of his own little snubnosed revolver and bought peace the way Lahey had. The note in the typewriter simply read, "I am most regretful for the policeman and his family—but I do, please believe me, regret it all."

I picked up his phone and called San Bernardino, got through to the homicide bureau, asked the guy there, "Does Captain Waring come in this early?"

"Not usually," was the reply, "but I think he's here this morning. Who's calling?"

I told him who was calling and he said "oh" and a moment later Waring came on. I told him what I'd found and I told him why I thought I'd found it and I read him the note.

"Sounds like a confession," Waring commented. "But what do you want me to do? You need to call LAPD."

"You call them for me," I suggested. "I called you because it's your case and because you told me yesterday that it's closed."

"I mis-spoke," he told me. "I was referring to the case against the deputy marshals."

"Well, you can close it for real now," I said.

"Maybe. But your judge did not kill Alfred Johansen."

"How can you be sure of that?"

"Because we have the man who did it. Or rather we have his remains in our morgue. It's shaping up as a classic contract job. The hitman himself was hit after the fact, and you know why."

I knew why, sure. And it was classical, all right. When would these suckers ever learn that their payoff usually comes as a bullet to the brain?

I asked Waring, "How do you know you have the right man?"

"We have the physical evidence—address found on the body, the knife, bloodstained handkerchief that was used to wipe the knife and a bloodmatch with the victim. We have the right man."

I sighed and told him, "I want to come in and talk to you."

"Any time," the captain said.

"Lahey was killed in the line of duty."

"We'll see."

I said, "No, bullshit, we won't see. He was killed while investigating these murders, suspended or no, so the man died on duty."

"Come in and talk to us, Joe."

I could do that. Sure, I could do that now. And it was time to come in from the dark.

CHAPTER 31

THE PROBLEM FOR me throughout had been too many actors upon the stage, too many playwrights behind the scenes, and too many stories within stories—and I'm speaking not of La Mancha but of Copp in the Dark. La Mancha was designed that way. Copp in the Dark, I think, just happened that way. In *Man of La Mancha* Craig who was really Alfie portrayed Cervantes who portrayed Quijana who fantasized himself as Quixote. Elaine Suzanne whose real name is Somoza portrayed an ugly female prisoner transformed by Cervantes into Aldonza, a sexy barmaid who in turn is transformed by Quixote into Dulcinea, the fairest of them all, and every actor in the play is portraying multiple roles. It is a transformational play and, in the end, the audience itself is transformed by the power of its message.

On the threatrical stage, it *is* powerful stuff.

Offstage, however, down here where most of us are staggering about in the dark much of our lives anyway, this kind of confusion only compounds the darkness and often results in tragedy.

We'd had plenty of that, all right, while Copp was in

the dark—and that was not just because I was in the dark but because everyone was to one extent or another.

Craig Maan, the gifted actor with the power to transform audiences, was in reality Alfred "Alfie" Johansen, son of a Minnesota Supreme Court justice and supposed student of chemical engineering who instead had majored in drama and thus had conned his father the judge out of nearly three years of an expensive college education.

But that was not the whole con. Alfie also was a closet gay and sometimes transvestite who'd fallen in with a shady crowd while still a student in Chicago. Caught in an FBI sweep of Chicago organized crime elements and sure to be exposed and scandalized at home, Alfie had thrown himself on the mercy of the FBI agent in charge of the operation and promised to deliver incriminating evidence on other crime figures while working undercover as an informant for the FBI.

The deal was struck and Alfie delivered—for awhile—and somehow he became entangled with the West Coast operations of Vin DiCenza who was already on trial in Los Angeles. Through this contact he had picked up hints that DiCenza already had Judge White in his pocket, and he relayed this information to his contact in the FBI.

The FBI then actively entered that angle and helped engineer an "in" for Alfie close to DiCenza. I believe that it was at this point that Alfie began to sniff a jackpot somewhere for himself and he began playing a double-agent role, trying to play both ends against the middle in the hope of parlaying a grand slam for himself.

Apparently, DiCenza was not all that comfortable in his accommodation with Judge White. He was no dummy so of course he knew about the judge's daughter, undoubtedly knew of her connection with his own son—(perhaps this was even his hold on the judge)—and he had Alfie under his wing, a gifted actor. I believe it began as Alfie's idea that he be positioned in close association with the judge's daughter "to keep an eye on things." The wily DiCenza, well schooled in Mafia symbology, quickly picked up on that idea but with a different slant: he would position Alfie next to the daughter and then *tell Judge White that he had done so* as a not-so-subtle message that the judge had best keep in line and deliver.

So Vin sent Alfie to Jimmy and Jimmy sent him to Judith who did not need a twisted arm to go for the guy. Meanwhile Vin's long arm had reached through San Francisco to make an offer that Greg Houston, already cast in *La Mancha*, could not refuse—and the blocks all slipped neatly into place.

Pursuing his double game, Alfie then reported his new position to the FBI who already were watching the trial very closely. The FBI instructed Alfie to hang in there and stay in touch and he did so, biding his time and alert to any and all developments that could be turned to his own advantage.

I believe the first development came when he finally succeeded in coming face to face with the judge. Something sparked there and Alfie knew it, he pursued it, and Alfie and the judge became an item, undercover of course. Love, you know, can cloud the mind—and homosexual love is no different in that regard. This guy Alfie was not only a gifted actor, he was a gifted con man too, so maybe he could convince a love-smitten judge that he would never betray him even though the judge had known up front that Alfie worked for DiCenza.

The judge became nervous about Alfie coming regularly to his condo, though, so he gave Alfie money to rent an apartment convenient to Alfie, and the judge began going to Alfie in disguise, dressed in drag—and maybe that was even a lot of fun for both of them. But note the twist on names again: Alfie rented the apartment in the name of the judge's dead wife. I talked to Lunceford about this doubleplay name business and maybe he had an insight there. Lunceford told me he thought Alfie hung his own name on Lunceford because he was afraid of dying incognito and no one would have known that he'd lived and died. A violent death would have brought the truth out with the real name closeby. I don't know. Myself, I think the guy just loved to play those kind of games and couldn't resist macabre little touches.

It was a perfect situation for the compulsive con man, though, and he of course was looking for ways to exploit it.

But then the judge got even more nervous about Alfie, checked him out, probably discovered then—to his horror—that Alfie had ties not only to the mob but to the FBI as well.

Enter, then, Dobbs and Harney, under instructions from the judge to protect his daughter and also to learn all they could about Alfie's true role and connections—and that was a dangerous game for the judge in itself, shows you how desperate the guy had become.

The rest was almost inevitable, certainly predictable.

The judge probably passed word to DiCenza that Alfie was on the FBI payroll and demanded that either DiCenza extract Alfie from the equation or their deal was off. Vin obviously did not know of the homosexual relationship between the two and he probably figured that he had all he needed out of Alfie anyway—so he ordered him hit.

Meanwhile Alfie had been forging ahead with his own mad scheme. He'd convinced Dobbs and Harney that he'd been assigned by the FBI to keep an eye on Judith White and that was his only involvement. But he hinted also that someone else in the cast was working for the mob, and he had these two hardened lawmen chasing their own tails around; God knows how many "disinformational spins" he had those guys in before they got to me.

They got to me through Alfie too, of course, but not by his design. They got to me by merely watching Alfie and his co-conspirators. Alfie was setting up a blackmail scheme, intending to bleed the judge for everything he had, and he'd conned the kids from *La Mancha* to assist him in that by leading them to believe that he would use the money to bankroll them all into bigtime theater.

Sanchez, Stein and Peterson were central to that scheme. These guys were into every kink in the sexual repertoire and had absolutely no qualms about setting any stage under Alfie's direction. The idea, I think, was for the judge to meet Alfie as usual at the blind apartment—maybe under the pretext of talking things out and making amends, whatever—and then Alfie was to lure the judge to the other apartment where the trap would be sprung under the watchful eye of a video camera and with a P.I. right next door ready to enter on cue and bear witness to the compromising scene. I believe he was setting the judge up for a homosexual orgy, all on tape and certainly destructive to everything the judge held dear. Don't know why he thought he needed me for that except as a melodramatic touch designed to really scare the judge, and I still have not made up my mind as to why he sent someone to my gym to get a nude picture of me. Maybe he'd intended a bit of blackmail against me too, just to keep me in line and cooperative.

Maybe it would have worked and maybe not, but obviously Alfie was confident enough in his attraction to the judge to feel that it would work. But something went terribly awry with the plan—I think possibly due to the marshals' activities, partly to mine, partly to DiCenza's, and partly to blind fate.

Instead of the judge showing up at the blind apartment, DiCenza's hitman took his place. This may have been by design. Whatever, the hitman killed Alfie and made it look like a sex crime. Maybe the nude photo of me had been there under the sofa cushion for awhile and just happened to play that way—or maybe the hitman found it in the apartment and used it as another set for the sexcrime angle. Whatever and however, Elaine became confused and delivered me to the wrong apartment—I believe she'd been there before and had a key—where we both discovered the crime but more to Elaine's consternation than mine. I've found no record of a marriage between her and Alfie; I think it was pure fluff.

I don't know how Dobbs and Harney got onto Elaine but after all they are professionals, maybe they had my house staked out, anyway they snatched her and grilled her and she took them back to the trap apartment. We know that because it's on the tape. Those guys kicked their way in there and probably had a field day with those kids—maybe not exactly with mayhem in mind but intending only to inflict pain and fear in the search for truth.

A thing like that can easily get out of hand and someone,

maybe Elaine, died in the process—and with that the die was cast for the rest of them. I think the marshals panicked and left there in a hell of a mental state after covering up the first perhaps accidental death with three more on purpose and intended to look just the way it did look. Panicky, yeah, and that's why they missed the videocassette—and that is why they missed Susan Baker. She'd gone over there to find out why I hadn't shown, was in the bathroom when Dobbs and Harney arrived, and spent the entire time hiding in a bedroom closet of that blood-spattered apartment, heard the whole gruesome encounter, ventured out only after all became quiet and spent the balance of the night pacing the floor in her own apartment, trying to contact Alfie and wondering what to do.

Judge White killed Art Lahey, sure.

He'd gone to the theater that night to see Judith, very concerned about the murders and probably feeling very threatened, probably intended to tell her the truth about his relationship with Alfie and beg not only her understanding but also her support in case things went sour for him. But Art Lahey and I were standing outside on the patio engrossed in conversation when he arrived; maybe he knew who one or both of us were and maybe he just overheard enough to know that the thing was falling apart. Remember the little old lady who asked me if Lahey and I were discussing the next play? Maybe someone else was listening, too, and maybe that someone panicked and followed Lahey out to his car, slugged him, then put Lahey's revolver in his mouth and pulled the trigger.

The judge probably left in a panic after that, drove around or killed time somewhere trying to figure out what to do next, called Judith and asked her to meet him after the show. Judith was very protective of her father, knew that something was wrong, didn't want me involved in it, no way. I don't believe he told her the whole story but maybe enough to make her wonder after she learned of Lahey's death.

She tried to drown the wonder in sex with me but it wouldn't hold, so later that night she went to see him, had it out with him, maybe learned the whole truth. And I think that is when the judge sucked up his own gun barrel.

Well, it's always good to come up into the light, even if what you see there is not exactly pretty.

There was some talk early on about a mistrial in the DiCenza case but I guess there will not be one. Another judge has been assigned and there has been a continuance of the sentencing phase. All the smart money now is saying that there will be no deal and that Vin will die in jail. That's okay with me, of course, everyone dies somewhere and a guy like Vin DiCenza was made for prison bars—and I guess it'll be okay, too, for a lot of nervous politicians who no doubt will go right on, now, enriching themselves at the public troughs.

I've heard no seamy scandals on Judge White yet, but of course there is endless speculation about his reasons for murdering a police officer and I guess the rest can't be far behind, the usual stories in the sensational press about murder conspiracies and hints that all was not clean in the judge's past. Actually it's already starting. A local TV station did a news feature the other day on the federal court system and judicial abuses, obviously trying to link Judge White's suicide with a recent spate of senate impeachments of federal judges back east somewhere.

See, these guys are not gods, they're not even perfect

human beings, and at the bottom line they are politicians—so what can you expect of an inverse system? You can pay them what they're worth, show them the proper respect, and watch them like hawks—then hope that the cream will find its proper place at the top of the bottle. What else can you do?

Dobbs and Harney are back in jail and the San Bernardino prosecutor is re-examining the evidence against them in the "unsolved" murders of Elaine Somoza, Jesus Sanchez, James Peterson and Peter Stein. I believe they'll take the fall like men, cop a plea on extenuating circumstances, and hope for a softhearted judge. They could even draw one count of involuntary manslaughter and three of second-degree murder, and maybe they'll get off with seven to ten in the slammer and an early parole. I'm due to go in tomorrow and give a deposition, and you already know what I'm going to say to the prosecutor.

Art Lahey's death has been officially upgraded to "line of duty" status, and that's good for his family. The good do sometimes die young, you know, but how do we know for sure that death is always a sort of punishment?—maybe sometimes it's a reward for good behavior, an early release like parole from the troubles of earth, a return with honors to the bliss of dreamtime. I'd buy that idea, for guys like Art Lahey.

Susan Baker has already told her story to the prosecutor and she's working something out that will allow her to go to Japan next month with a show—following her karma, I guess, still in pursuit of the unreachable star. Maybe she'll even find it between her thighs, where she's been looking all the while anyway.

Lunceford told me that he's abandoning the dream. He's

very young and feeling very heavily the burdens of family responsibilities, and his father-in-law wants to take him into his general contracting business but it involves travel so he'll have to give up the theater, and he says that is what he is going to do. Way I see it, that doesn't have to mean the end of dreams. What is wrong with wanting to be the best damned builder in the country, or the best plumber or carpenter or shopkeeper? Dreams can be anywhere the lifeline takes us; maybe we shouldn't try to narrow it down so much.

Justice Johansen came in from Minnesota a couple of days ago to take his boy home. Tried to give me some more money but hell he probably needs it more than I do and I did nothing to earn it. Told me that he'd never had an inkling that Alfie wanted to study drama. He'd hoped that his son would want to go to law school and was very surprised when Alfie opted for chemical engineering—said he wouldn't have objected to him studying theater arts, so it's a strange world. I didn't tell the judge anything about Alfie's ignoble pursuits. He thinks his kid was killed in the line of undercover duty with the FBI, so he'll have to learn otherwise from someone other than me.

Actually brought a smile to the judge's face when I told him that Alfie seemed to have an interest in law and that he would have made a good lawyer. Of course, I didn't qualify "good" and I think maybe Johansen's smile was tinged with irony.

I haven't seen Judith since last Saturday. The theater is dark and apparently will stay that way until a new producer can lighten it again. But every time I pass that corner, for the rest of my life, I will think of *Man of La Mancha* and the quest for excellence in human affairs.

That's not such a bad thing to think about, not even for a Copp for Hire.

Lunceford told me that Judith left town even before her father's funeral.

Said he thinks she went to New Zealand.

Maybe I'll wander down that way too, some day soon, if my Visa can stand it. I dream sometimes, too, you know. And I'll never stop dreaming of Judy, impossible though it may be.

Impossible, you see, because I believe with all my heart and mind that Judith White pulled the trigger on her father.

Don Pendleton is the author of the bestselling series, The Executioner. He resides in La Verne, CA.

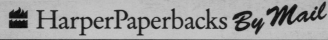

HarperPaperbacks *By Mail*

EXPLOSIVE THRILLERS FROM THREE BESTSELLING AUTHORS

LEN DEIGHTON

Spy Sinker

British agent Bernard Samson, the hero of *Spy Hook* and *Spy Line*, returns for a final bow in this thrilling novel. Through terrible treachery, Samson is betrayed by the one person he least suspects—his lovely wife, Fiona.

Spy Story

Pat Armstrong is an expert at computer generated tactical war games. But when he returns to his old apartment to find that someone who looks just like him has taken over his identity, he is thrust into an international conspiracy that is all too real.

Catch a Falling Spy

On the parched sands of the Sahara desert, Andrei Bekuv, a leading Russian scientist, defects, setting off a shadow war between the KGB and the CIA. Yet, nothing is what it seems—least of all, Bekuv's defection.

BERNARD CORNWELL

Crackdown

Drug pirates stalk their victims in the treacherous waters of the Bahamas, then return to their fortress island of Murder Cay. Then comes skipper Nicholas Breakspear with the son and daughter of a U.S. Senator. What should have been a simple de-tox cruise soon lurches into a voyage of terror and death as Breakspear is lured into a horrifying plot of cocaine, cash, and killings.

Killer's Wake

Suspected of sailing off with a valuable family treasure, sea gypsy John Rossendale must return to England to face his accusing relatives. But in the fog-shrouded waters of the Channel Islands, Rossendale, alone and unarmed, is plunged into someone's violent game of cat-and-mouse where a lot more is at stake than family relations.

CAMPBELL ARMSTRONG

Agents of Darkness

Suspended from the LAPD, Charlie Galloway decides his life has no meaning. But when his Filipino housekeeper is murdered, Charlie finds a new purpose in tracking the killer. He never expects, though, to be drawn into a conspiracy that reaches from the Filipino jungles to the White House.

Mazurka

For Frank Pagan of Scotland Yard, it begins with the murder of a Russian at crowded Waverly Station, Edinburgh. From that moment on, Pagan's life becomes an ever-darkening nightmare as he finds himself trapped in a complex web of intrigue, treachery, and murder.

Mambo

Super-terrorist Gunther Ruhr has been captured. Scotland Yard's Frank Pagan must escort him to a maximum security prison, but with blinding swiftness and brutality, Ruhr escapes. Once again, Pagan must stalk Ruhr, this time into an earth-shattering secret conspiracy.

Brainfire

American John Rayner is a man on fire with grief and anger over the death of his powerful brother. Some say it was suicide, but Rayner suspects something more sinister. His suspicions prove correct as he becomes trapped in a Soviet-made maze of betrayal and terror.

Asterisk Destiny

Asterisk is America's most fragile and chilling secret. It waits somewhere in the Arizona desert to pave the way to world domination...or damnation. Two men, White House aide John Thorne and CIA agent Ted Hollander, race to crack the wall of silence surrounding Asterisk and tell the world of their terrifying discovery.

MAIL TO: **Harper Collins Publishers**
P. O. Box 588 Dunmore, PA 18512-0588
OR CALL: (800) 331-3761 (Visa/MasterCard)

Yes, please send me the books I have checked:

☐ SPY SINKER (0-06-109928-7) $5.95
☐ SPY STORY (0-06-100265-8) $4.99
☐ CATCH A FALLING SPY (0-06-100207-0) $4.95
☐ CRACKDOWN (0-06-109924-4) $5.95
☐ KILLER'S WAKE (0-06-100046-9) $4.95
☐ AGENTS OF DARKNESS (0-06-109944-9) $5.99
☐ MAZURKA (0-06-100010-8) $4.95
☐ MAMBO (0-06-109902-3) $5.95
☐ BRAINFIRE (0-06-100086-8) $4.95
☐ ASTERISK DESTINY (0-06-100160-0) $4.95

SUBTOTAL .... $________

POSTAGE AND HANDLING .... $ 2.00*

SALES TAX (Add applicable sales tax) .... $________

TOTAL: $________

*(ORDER 4 OR MORE TITLES AND POSTAGE & HANDLING IS FREE! Orders of less than 4 books, please include $2.00 p/h. Remit in US funds, do not send cash.)

Name ________________

Address ________________

City ________________

State ________ Zip ________

(Valid only in US & Canada)

Allow up to 6 weeks delivery.
Prices subject to change.

HO271